❊ Tim took a deep breath and sent energy through his being. *Cat*, he thought, *I am a cat. I have whiskers and a tail and four paws.* He pictured himself in cat form, imagined cat moves, thought about basic catness.

He forced himself not to panic as he felt a transformation taking place in his body. His face flattened, his ears moved to the top of his head. His skin tingled, as if electricity ran through his veins instead of blood.

While his body dramatically altered shape, Tim could feel inner changes as well. His senses all heightened, smells and sounds sending shivers of excitement through him. His thoughts about the past and the future seemed to melt away, his only interest in the *right now*.

Uh oh, he thought. *This transformation may be a little more complete than I anticipated.*

Don't lose yourself completely, he warned himself. *You're going to need to remember who you are and how you did this, so that you can turn back into yourself again.*

"You are Tim Hunter!" he declared. Only it came out as a loud "Mrrroooowww!"

Tim's eyes burst open. He stared down and saw paws. *Paws!*

He'd done it. He was a cat! ❊

the BOOKS of MAGIC ™ 6

Reckonings

Carla Jablonski

Created by
Neil Gaiman and John Bolton

BOOKS FOR
VERTIGO
YOUNG ADULTS

EOS

An Imprint of HarperCollinsPublishers

Eos is an imprint of HarperCollins Publishers.

Timothy Hunter and *The Books of Magic* created by Neil Gaiman and John Bolton.

The Books of Magic: Reckonings was primarily adapted from the story serialized
in *The Books of Magic: Reckonings*; *The Books of Magic: Transformations*; *The
Books of Magic: Girl in the Box*; *The Books of Magic: Death After Death*; and
The Books of Faerie, originally published by Vertigo, an imprint of DC Comics,
© 1996, 1997, 1998, 1999, and 2001.

The Books of Magic: Reckonings, Transformations, Girl in the Box, and *Death After
Death* comic books were created by the following people:

Written by John Ney Reiber
Illustrated by Peter Gross

The Books of Faerie were created by the following people:

Written by Bronwyn Carlton and John Ney Reiber
Illustrated by Peter Gross

Library of Congress Cataloging-in-Publication Data
Jablonski, Carla.
    Reckonings / by Carla Jablonski ; created by Neil Gaiman and John Bolton.—
1st Eos ed.
        p.   cm. (Books of magic ; #6)
    "Primarily adapted from the story serialized in The Books of Magic: Reckonings;
The Books of Magic: Transformations; The Books of Magic: Girl in the Box; The
Books of Magic: Death After Death; and The Books of Faerie, originally published
by Vertigo, an imprint of DC Comics, 1996, 1997, 1998, 1999, and 2001"—
Copyright page.
    Summary: Concerned that he might become evil and endanger his girlfriend in
the future, thirteen-year-old Timothy Hunter returns to Faerie to get the truth
about his parentage and his magic once and for all.
    ISBN 0-06-447384-8 (pbk.)
    [1. Magic—Fiction.   2. Wizards—Fiction.]   I. Gaiman, Neil   II. Bolton, John,
1951–   III. Title.
PZ7.J1285Re 2004   2003023029
[Fic]—dc22

❖

First Eos edition, 2004
Visit us on the World Wide Web!
www.harpereos.com
www.dccomics.com

For Neil,
where the magic all began,
with thanks.
—CJ

THE BOOKS OF MAGIC
An Introduction

by Neil Gaiman

WHEN I WAS STILL a teenager, only a few years older than Tim Hunter is in the book you are holding, I decided it was time to write my first novel. It was to be called *Wild Magic*, and it was to be set in a minor British Public School (which is to say, a private school), like the ones from which I had so recently escaped, only a minor British Public School that taught magic. It had a young hero named Richard Grenville, and a pair of wonderful villains who called themselves Mister Croup and Mister Vandemar. It was going to be a mixture of Ursula K. Le Guin's *A Wizard of Earthsea* and T. H. White's *The Sword in the Stone*, and, well, me, I suppose. That was the plan. It seemed to me that learning about magic was the perfect story, and I was sure I could really write convincingly about school.

I wrote about five pages of the book before I realized that I had absolutely no idea what I was doing, and I stopped. (Later, I learned that most books are actually written by people who have no idea what they are doing, but go on to finish writing the books anyway. I wish I'd known that then.)

Years passed. I got married, and had children of my own, and learned how to finish writing the things I'd started.

Then one day in 1988, the telephone rang.

It was an editor in America named Karen Berger. I had recently started writing a monthly comic called *The Sandman*, which Karen was editing, although no issues had yet been published. Karen had noticed that I combined a sort of trainspotterish knowledge of minor and arcane DC Comics characters with a bizarre facility for organizing them into something more or less coherent. And also, she had an idea.

"Would you write a comic," she asked, "that would be a history of magic in the DC Comics universe, covering the past and the present and the future? Sort of a Who's Who, but with a story? We could call it *The Books of Magic*."

I said, "No, thank you." I pointed out to her how silly an idea it was—a Who's Who and a history and a travel guide that was also a story. "Quite a ridiculous idea," I said, and she apologized for having suggested it.

In bed that night I hovered at the edge of sleep, musing about Karen's call, and what a ridiculous idea it was. I mean . . . a story that would go from the beginning of time . . . to the end of time . . . and have someone meet all these strange people . . . and learn all about magic. . . .

Perhaps it wasn't so ridiculous. . . .

And then I sighed, certain that if I let myself sleep it would all be gone in the morning. I climbed out of bed and crept through the house back to my office, trying not to wake anyone in my hurry to start scribbling down ideas.

A boy. Yes. There had to be a boy. Someone smart and funny, something of an outsider, who would learn that he had the potential to be the greatest magician the world had ever seen—more powerful than Merlin. And four guides, to take him through the past, the present, through other worlds, through the future, serving the same function as the ghosts who accompany Ebenezer Scrooge through Charles Dickens's *A Christmas Carol.*

I thought for a moment about calling him Richard Grenville, after the hero of my book-I'd-never-written, but that seemed a rather too heroic name (the original Sir Richard Grenville was a sea captain, adventurer, and explorer, after all). So I called him Tim, possibly because the Monty

Python team had shown that Tim was an unlikely sort of name for an enchanter, or with faint memories of the hero of Margaret Storey's magical children's novel, *Timothy and Two Witches*. I thought perhaps his last name should be Seekings, and it was, in the first outline I sent to Karen—a faint tribute to John Masefield's haunting tale of magic and smugglers, *The Midnight Folk*. But Karen felt this was a bit literal, so he became, in one stroke of the pen, Tim Hunter.

And as Tim Hunter he sat up, blinked, wiped his glasses on his T-shirt, and set off into the world.

(I never actually got to use the minor British Public School that taught only magic in a story, and I suppose now I never will. But I was very pleased when Mr. Croup and Mr. Vandemar finally showed up in a story about life under London, called *Neverwhere*.)

John Bolton, the first artist to draw Tim, had a son named James who was just the right age and he became John's model for Tim, tousle-haired and bespectacled. And in 1990 the first four volumes of comics that became the first *Books of Magic* graphic novel were published.

Soon enough, it seemed, Tim had a monthly series of comics chronicling his adventures and misadventures, and the slow learning process he was to undergo, as initially chronicled by author John Ney Reiber, who gave Tim a number of things—most importantly, Molly.

In this new series of novels-without-pictures, Carla Jablonski has set herself a challenging task: not only adapting Tim's stories, but also telling new ones, and through it all illuminating the saga of a young man who might just grow up to be the most powerful magician in the world. If, of course, he manages to live that long. . . .

Neil Gaiman
May 2002

Prologue

ONCE UPON A TIME, there was a beautiful queen who presided with her king over the land of Faerie. She enjoyed being queen, reveling in her luxuries and Magicks, the beauty of the land and her court. But being queen can be very lonely. Her husband, Auberon, had married her to form an alliance. Perhaps he loved her a little; she loved him sometimes. But she never forgot that her real value to him was political. That and his hope that she would produce an heir and thus ensure the royal line.

And while Titania had company at all times, she had no true friends. With so much gossip and intrigue at court, how could she confide in anyone there? She had often relied on her courtier Amadan, but she wasn't sure if she could trust him. He'd turn up in the oddest places, as if he'd been eavesdropping or spying. She didn't think he was reporting back to her husband, for Auberon seemed easily irritated by the tiny creature, but Amadan had an agenda at all times—that much she could see.

Still, Amadan had stood her in good stead when she first became queen. She was not royalty by birth. She had been thrust into royal life unprepared; it was Amadan who taught her, counseled her, protected her. But an obsequious flitling was not a true friend. And there was nowhere she felt that she could just be herself.

So she began to visit the world of the humans. The gates were always open; it was easy to do and easy to hide her Faeriness beneath glamours that gave her skin the human hue. The unfamiliar landscape and the promise of uninterrupted time alone made her feel free. Free enough to sit and weep for her family whom she had left behind when she moved to the court, for her lonely heart, for her thwarted romantic dreams.

"Sorrowing lady, why do you cry? What may I do to help you?"

Those were Tamlin's first words to her. Tamlin, perhaps the handsomest human she had ever seen. He was nearly as beautiful as the Fair Folk. "Don't be afraid," he said. "My name is Tamlin, and I would never harm you."

"I—I think I'd better go back now," Titania stammered, feeling as foolish as a young child. He set her heart racing, and it frightened her. She wanted to get away from him, and yet she didn't want to let him go. She stood. "Yes, I must go back."

"Then let me escort you," Tamlin insisted. "These woods are no place for a woman alone. Let me come with you to your home."

"You wish to come to where I live?" Titania asked. "Of your own free will?" An idea was forming in her head.

"Of course," Tamlin replied.

"Come then, Tamlin. Of your own volition, come with me."

And so she brought the human to Faerie, knowing as she did so that he could never return to the land of his birth. Visit, yes. But he would always have to return to her as her willing prisoner.

Willing because before long they fell in love, and Tamlin did not ever want to leave her side. She taught him certain Magicks—shape-shifing, for example, and herbal remedies—and they spent many happy days and nights together.

But their happiness couldn't last. Tamlin was furious that Titania would not leave her husband for him. She refused to give up her Faerie kingdom in order to be with him openly. When she announced that she was pregnant, and that the child would be the King's heir, Tamlin angrily reminded her that she could not know who the child's father really was. Was he the father, or was Auberon? Would the child be all

Faerie, or would human blood also course through his veins?

Titania hid her fear of the consequences and sent Tamlin away. She did not want to lose her title, her position. Even if the child were his, she would never tell him. It would give him too much power over her; he would have too many rights to claim. Perhaps, even if the child were Tamlin's, Auberon would never have to know. The child might take after her, after all. It might yet appear to be a true child of Faerie. She could train the human nature right out of him if necessary.

Yet, to be safe, she secretly asked Amadan to hire a special nurse for her—one who could be trusted. And on that fateful day, with King Auberon away, she bore her child . . . a child with obvious marks of humanity.

"This child's existence will be a threat to you as long as you live," Amadan warned her. "You could be tried for treason for your infidelity. This child is the proof of it."

"What can I do?" she asked.

"What you must. That is, if you value your throne."

"Yes," Titania murmured. "Yes. Do it."

The nurse took the pink and healthy baby boy from the Queen's arms. "I have always been reliable," the nurse said. "You can count on me." She wrapped the baby in her cloak and left the room.

"We will inform the King and the court that the child was born dead," Amadan said. "It will not be a lie for long."

Tears trickled from Titania's eyes. "Please. Leave me alone."

Amadan bowed, and flitted out the window.

The sad Queen stared out the window at the night sky. "Oh, Tamlin," she moaned. "What have I done? Now you will never forgive me. I may never forgive myself."

Days went by. Auberon grieved and consoled his unhappy wife in her loss. Amadan hovered, and watched to keep Tamlin away.

But Tamlin had followed the nurse into the woods. He was astonished when she and the baby disappeared into a misty portal. There was no proof that she ever did what she had set out to do; she certainly did not return. He never said a word to Titania. She had wanted to be rid of the child—his child—so what would be the point? He stopped coming to her door, stopped yearning for her so keenly.

And despite everything, Titania was convinced that her son was alive. Somewhere.

Chapter One

TIMOTHY HUNTER WINCED AS Molly O'Reilly's mother launched into a tirade.

"I've told you to stop calling," Mrs. O'Reilly snapped on the other end of the phone line. "Molly is not allowed to speak to you. And if you ring again, I'll be speaking to your father about it."

Mrs. O'Reilly's cold fury came through the phone with such intensity that Tim imagined icicles forming along the line. He forced the thought aside. Being magic, he had learned that sometimes if he imagined something, it could actually happen. The last thing he needed was to have to explain to his exasperated, irritated, melancholy dad how the phone froze.

"Have I made myself quite clear, young man?" Mrs. O'Reilly demanded.

"But—" Tim began to protest, then stopped

himself. Mrs. O'Reilly was being unreasonable, but for him to say so would only get him and Molly in deeper trouble. Adults hated it when they were corrected by thirteen-year-olds. He and Molly were in deep enough as it was.

"*But?*" Mrs. O'Reilly repeated, the word coming out as with frosty and incredulous admonishment.

Tim cringed. *You really need to learn to keep your mouth shut*, he told himself.

"How dare you try to defend yourself to me, Timothy Hunter," she scolded.

If he'd had any doubt before, he knew he was in trouble for sure now. Molly's mom usually liked him, and she only used his whole name if she was particularly angry or horribly worried. Like the time he was eight years old and she had been taking care of him and Molly, and he had managed to knock himself out on the swing set. She had called him "Timothy Hunter" then, too.

"After keeping my daughter out all night," she exploded, "without any explanation! Lord knows what the two of you got up to—"

"Nothing!" Tim blurted. "We didn't do anything wrong, I swear."

Mrs. O'Reilly snorted. "That may be true. Then again, maybe not. So *leave Molly alone.*"

Slam went the phone. Tim replaced the receiver glumly. "Well, that was less than useless," he muttered.

He trudged back up to his room and flopped onto his unmade bed. He'd never been in so much trouble before—not even when he skipped out of school in the middle of gym class. He was also pretty certain that Molly's parents had never been so mad at her. And it was all his fault. Well, not exactly *his* fault. More precisely, it was *magic's* fault!

Tim's whole world had tilted ever since he'd discovered he was magic. And not just magic—he had the potential to become the most powerful magician ever. Which was part of the problem. This possibility made all kinds of other magical sorts—demons, for instance—much too interested in Tim and his future. In fact, Tim had discovered that there was a whole set of powerful creatures who wanted to make sure he didn't *have* a future. This was what had gotten him and Molly into so much trouble. Molly had been kidnapped and whisked off to the Demon Playland. Tim couldn't quite put his finger on why, but he knew that Molly had been kidnapped by demons because of him. It took a while for them to escape, and that was what had kept them away overnight.

Molly's parents had gone ballistic, and she

had been grounded. *More like placed under house arrest*, Tim thought. Demons were a lot less scary than Molly's furious parents, Tim had discovered, and even though magic had gotten them into this mess, it wasn't going to get them out of it. At least, no magic that Tim could think of.

Tim reached over and grabbed a ball that sat on the floor. He rolled onto his back and tossed the ball from hand to hand. He'd been grounded, too, but his dad hadn't been quite so fanatical about it. Tim wondered if that was partly because his dad wasn't his real dad. That was another one of the whammies hurled his way along with the magic. Tim's real dad was a bloke called Tamlin who had lived in another world entirely, a world called Faerie.

Tim began bouncing the ball against the wall and catching it. *Thwump*. Catch. *Thwump*. Catch. It made a satisfying rhythm.

Then again, Tim thought. *Thwump*. Catch. *Maybe dear old "Dad" didn't even notice I was gone*.

When Tim had arrived home that morning, Mr. Hunter hadn't even been there. He'd been sitting in the wrecked car that he kept in a parking lot several streets over. The car was so damaged it would never run again, but Mr. Hunter still hung on to it. He would go sit in it sometimes on his seriously bad days. Mr. Hunter had been at the wheel of that very same car when he'd gotten into the accident that had killed Tim's mum and had left Mr. Hunter with only one arm. Tim called the car the Guiltmobile.

So it was perfectly possible that Mr. Hunter had spent the night slumped in the Guiltmobile and never even noticed that Tim had been gone the whole time. When Mrs. O'Reilly came over to scream bloody murder at everyone within hearing distance, Mr. Hunter had been pretty mild about it all. His response had been, "Kids will be kids, and these are a pair of good ones." That made Mrs. O'Reilly madder.

"Don't you take that boys-will-be-boys attitude with me, William Hunter."

"That's not what I—" Mr. Hunter had protested, but Mrs. O'Reilly's sour face shut him up.

So then Mr. Hunter agreed to punish Tim as well. Not only was Tim grounded, his skateboard had also been confiscated.

That was two days ago. Since then Mr. Hunter had barely spoken to Tim. Tim had a feeling his dad was probably afraid that Mrs. O'Reilly thought he wasn't a fit parent. Or maybe Mr. Hunter was annoyed that he'd gotten yelled at for something that Tim had done.

To make things worse, spring holiday had just started, so he and Molly wouldn't even get a chance to see each other at school. And he needed to see her, to talk to her about all that was happening. Besides, everything was different now. They were officially boyfriend and girlfriend; they'd even kissed! More than once!

"Boyfriends and girlfriends are supposed to see each other," Tim grumbled, catching the ball again. "It's one of the rules."

He rolled off the bed and opened his bedroom door. The usual drone of the telly drifted upstairs. "Dad's down for the night," Tim surmised. Mr. Hunter spent a lot of time glued to the tube, particularly when some old black-and-white musical was on. "He'll never notice if I'm not in my room."

Tim grabbed his rain slicker, then took the stairs slowly, careful to avoid any possibly creaky boards. He held his breath and quickly passed the door to the living room, stopping for a moment to listen. His dad hadn't moved. _If I'm caught sneaking out, what's the worst he'll do? He wasn't that angry at me_, Tim told himself. _It was Mrs. O'Reilly who really riled him up. Besides, I'll be back in my room before he ever notices I'm gone._

Tim turned the doorknob, every muscle tense as he braced himself for squeaks, but the door swung open silently. _As if it wants me to go see Molly_, Tim decided. _Excellent._

Man, it sure is wet and dark out here. Molly only

lived a few streets over, but his sneakers were soaked almost instantly, making his socks squishy. By the time he reached Molly's house his hair was plastered to his head, and rain dripped from his glasses.

"Hi, Filthy," Tim greeted the gray cat perched on a nearby fence. Filthy was a stray Molly had adopted recently. "What are you doing out? I thought cats didn't like the rain."

The cat ignored Tim and continued gazing intently at the window above them. Another cat sat inside on the windowsill, dry and content, peering down.

Tim nodded knowingly. "Oh, I see. Well, if it's any consolation, I can't see my girlfriend either," Tim told the cat. "Mrs. O'Reilly made that really clear. If she won't even let me talk to Molly on the phone, there's no way she'd let me inside."

Filthy flicked his tail, his yellow eyes still on the calico above them.

"Too bad you can't go talk to Molly for me," Tim said, stroking the cat's wet gray fur. He grinned down at the critter, an idea forming.

Maybe magic can help me after all. He took a step away from the cat, studying it.

"Tamlin could turn himself into a falcon," Tim said. "Maybe shape-shifting is a skill that runs in the family. After all, he is my real dad."

Tim shut his eyes to help him concentrate. He reached out with his mind to Filthy, feeling the cat's shape, probing it for its essence. He didn't want to take over the cat's body; he wanted to learn it, understand it. Once he sensed with his deepest self what it meant to be a cat, he stopped focusing on Filthy and turned his attention inward.

"Tamlin made this look pretty easy," he murmured, "and he had all those feathers to keep track of."

He took a deep breath and sent energy through his being. *Cat*, he thought, *I am a cat. I have whiskers and a tail and four paws*. He pictured himself in cat form, imagined cat moves, thought about basic catness.

He forced himself not to panic as he felt a transformation taking place in his body. His face flattened, his ears moved to the top of his head. His skin tingled, as if electricity ran through his veins instead of blood. His center of gravity changed, causing him to tip forward, but he didn't fall—he landed on front paws.

Then his whole body felt one enormous unbearable itch, an itch to end all itches, and just as he thought his body would explode—fur sprang from his skin.

While his body dramatically altered shape,

Tim could feel inner changes as well. His senses all heightened, smells and sounds sending shivers of excitement through him. His thoughts about the past and the future seemed to melt away, his only interest in the *right now*.

Uh oh, he thought. *This transformation may be a little more complete than I anticipated.*

Don't lose yourself completely, he warned himself. *You're going to need to remember who you are and how you did this, so that you can turn back into yourself again.*

"You are Tim Hunter!" he declared. Only it came out as a loud "Mrrroooowww!"

Tim's eyes burst open. He stared down and saw paws. *Paws!*

He'd done it. He was a cat!

Chapter Two

"NOT BAD FOR A first try!" he cheered, making triumphant chirruping sounds.

His glasses tumbled onto the ground. *Cat's faces aren't built for glasses, I guess,* Tim thought. *The nose is too flat, and the ears are in the wrong place.* He blinked and realized he could see even better than he could wearing glasses. *Cats have such excellent vision. It's like being automatically fitted with contacts.*

A terrified cat yowl got his attention. "Filthy, what's wrong?" He was puzzled by Filthy's bared teeth and flattened ears. Tim leaned in closer and Filthy hissed at him.

Then Tim realized—he was looking at Filthy eye-to-eye—and Filthy was standing on top of a fence! Tim had turned himself into a cat all right—only he was still human size! No wonder the poor cat was freaking. Its fur was puffed out so that it was nearly as round as a balloon.

"So I made a minor miscalculation." Tim checked out Filthy again. The cat's back was arched like a creature in a Halloween cartoon. "Okay, not so minor, maybe. But, hey, give me a break! I took care of the hard part—I'm a cat, for cripe's sake. Getting the size right should be a breeze compared to starting from scratch!"

Tim concentrated again, thinking about shrinking, getting compact. His fur bristled, and he tingled all over once more. In moments, he and Filthy were the same size.

Filthy was still very wary. *I wonder if I don't smell quite right*, Tim wondered, as Filthy yowled and ran away. "Was it something I said?" Tim called after the disappearing cat. Only it came out as "Mrrrowrrr?"

Time to set the plan in motion, Tim determined.

Time? What's that? a voice in Tim's head asked. The voice sounded like Tim's, but it was softer and more languid.

Is time something good to eat? To chase? Soft to lie on? the voice asked.

"No, no, nothing like that," Tim replied. "Why are there two of us in here?"

Who are you? the voice asked. Tim noticed it rolled its *r*s, making a purring sound, and he began to get an inkling of what was going on.

"I'm me," Tim told the voice. "Thirteen-year-old boy magician."

Then who am I?

"Don't quote me on this, but I'm pretty sure you came with the body. You must be Cat. All cat."

That seemed to satisfy the voice. *When will you feed me?* Cat-Tim asked.

"Later. Right now we're going to visit Molly." He slunk toward Molly's back door.

Wet. There is too much wet, Cat-Tim thought.

"No kidding," Tim agreed.

I prefer my paws dry.

"They're not your paws," Tim argued, "they're my feet. And if they have to get wet, then they'll get wet."

Fine, the cat part of him acquiesced. *When are you going to feed me?*

"I told you. Later." Tim pushed through the little swinging cat door in the bottom panel of the back door.

That was an admirable slither. You're the greatest. Will you feed me now?

"Stop trying to butter me up. We're not here to eat, we're here to see Molly." He padded up the stairs to her room and slipped inside.

There's no one in here.

"I can see that," Tim snapped. Molly's room was even messier than Tim's, but despite the piles of clothes scattered across the floor, the books, notebooks, backpacks, and sneakers, Tim could see that the room was currently a Molly-free zone.

"Why isn't she here?" Tim knew that she'd been grounded just like he had—with probably even stricter rules. He figured her parents had not just placed her under house arrest but were forcing her to do time in solitary, trapped in her room.

Tim spotted the open window and the thick rope tied to Molly's bed. "She climbed out the window," he realized. "And I bet she went to see me! She's probably at my house right now, wondering where I am."

Cat-Tim yawned, making Tim wonder who was actually in charge of this shape. *Why would anyone want to go out on a nasty cold wet night like this?* Cat-Tim thought. The cat part of him compelled him to leap onto Molly's bed, unsheathe its claws, and begin kneading the comforter.

"Quit it," Tim ordered Cat-Tim. "We have to go find Molly." Seeing the rope assured him that she'd left the room on her own, at least. This didn't look like a demon-induced exit.

Cat-Tim's tail flicked in irritation. *But it's so nice and warm and dry in here, and there's a bowl of Yummy Treats on the floor!*

Tim used all his concentration and forced his cat body off the bed, down the stairs and back out the little swinging cat door. The rain pelted his fur, making him shiver.

This is a very silly thing to do. Running back and forth in the rain. Not even stopping for treats.

"Well, we're doing it anyway," Tim retorted. "Besides, those treats are for Filthy."

Why are you in charge?

"Because you're not even really a cat," Tim said. "You're just the shape I'm in." He shook his head. "Sheesh. I've spent most of my life arguing with myself, but it's never been anything like this!"

Tim padded down the wet streets, staying close to the walls, trying to sneak through the raindrops. His cat body really hated getting wet. Interesting smells from the tall garbage cans looming above him distracted his hungry cat stomach from time to time, but Tim managed to get his cat self back to his house quickly.

Only Molly wasn't there. Not out front, not in the back, not on the sidewalk trying to figure out a way in. Tim scrambled up a tree and peered into his window. She wasn't inside either.

I thought you said she was here.

"I thought she would be," Tim replied. If he still had a human face, he'd be frowning with disappointment. Molly was breaking serious rules by sneaking out. Who was she breaking them to see, if not him? What was she doing?

He dropped back down to the ground.

You have a lot to learn about landing. You call that a leap?

"Can you be quiet? I'm trying to decide what to do."

We have our nap and snack now. That's what we do. The cat's nose lifted into the air. *I smell hamburger over there.*

"Try sniffing around for Molly instead of food," Tim said.

I'm not a dog. I don't track. Besides—the cat lowered its face to the pavement—*there is no Molly smell here.*

"How am I going to find her? She could be anywhere."

We don't have to stay in the rain. The cat body bounded under a parked car. *This is better.*

"We're not going to find her under here," Tim protested. "We can't see anything but puddles!"

But we're dry.

"What we need is one of those newscaster helicopters, like they have on telly. We could get a view of the whole city and find her that way."

There's mud on my paws. I don't like dirt.

Tim felt suddenly inspired. "Be quiet," he ordered his cat self, as he formulated a plan. He crawled out from under the car. "I need to concentrate."

Don't tell me to—

"I mean it! Unless you want to wind up with wings on your tail!"

What?

Tim could sense the cat's utter astonishment, and took advantage of its momentary speechlessness. He sent a shiver of energy through his body, letting it settle along his spine. He visualized a pair of wings sprouting from his back. "Wings," he murmured. "I want wings."

He heard himself let out a wild, loud yowl, and poof! The next thing he knew, he was sporting a pair of strong wings.

He glanced around to peer at them. "Wow. I'm getting pretty good at this stuff," he commented.

Those are rodent wings, Cat-Tim complained.

"I guess so," Tim said. "Bat wings just kind of popped into my head."

How dare you put rodent wings on me! The cat wriggled its body, as if it could shake the wings off. All its fur puffed up in fury.

"Would you rather have bird wings?" Tim demanded. "They'd never hold us up. These babies will give us the bird's-eye view we need." He gave the wings a flap. They made a satisfying _whoosh_ sound.

"Okay, prepare for liftoff." He took a deep breath. "Airplanes zoom along the runway to get enough speed to take off. I'll try the same technique."

I can't talk you out of this?

"Nope." Tim looked up and down the empty street. The weather and time of night made it deserted: no pedestrians, no cars.

"We are cleared for takeoff. Ready . . ." Tim hunkered down, preparing to spring. "Set . . ." He wiggled his cat backside. "Go!" He leaped into action, racing down the center of the street. Midway up the block he began flapping his wings. He felt himself lifting off the ground. He flapped harder. Harder. Within moments, Tim was flying over the city.

"Whoo-hoo!" He gazed down at the amazing sight of the rain-soaked buildings, streets, and lights below him. "I'm a boy, a cat, and a bat all rolled into one. Talk about a split personality!"

Not in my wildest dreams—or nightmares . . . the cat-voice sputtered, unable to complete the thought.

Tim understood how the cat part of him felt. The magic of it all was nearly overwhelming. It was amazing and totally bizarre—and scary and exciting all at once. He flapped harder, and began his search for Molly.

* * *

A boy named Daniel, wearing the garb and the grime of a Victorian chimney sweep, sat on a London rooftop, not caring that it was raining. The gloom matched his mood perfectly.

"Oh, Marya," he sighed sadly, as he often did. "Why can't I forget about you? I just wants to make things right, but I don't know how."

He had never meant to harm Marya or to scare her, but that was exactly what he had done. After she'd left their world, Free Country, and decided to stay in this one, Daniel had thought he would go mad with missing her. So he had followed her here and made a right mess of things.

He clenched his fists and pounded his legs. "If only you hadn't been so jealous," he berated himself. But he had been, blinded by such rage that he had done foolish things. He had blamed that magician, Timothy Hunter, for stealing Marya away from him. He had tried to kill the bloke, in fact, and had lashed out at Marya, too.

Now that he'd been on his own for weeks, scrounging around London with no one to talk to and plenty of time on his hands, he realized how wrong he had been. About everything.

"I wonder if the poor blighter survived the tunnels," he muttered, shivering against the rain. All the magician had done was try to help him, and how had Daniel thanked him? By leaving Tim to drown in the underground tunnels, that's how. How could he ever face Marya after pulling a stunt like that? She'd hate him for sure, now. He had promised himself never to approach her again until he was good through and through, good enough for her. And he didn't know if he ever would be.

But it was so hard, knowing she was out there, somewhere. London itself was hard. He wanted to protect her, though he knew that she was probably faring far better than he was. She had friends. He had . . . what? Pigeons to fight for a patch of dry roof.

All he could do was picture her gentle, pretty face, and it ate him up, leaving him so empty inside that no food could fill him. It would be nice if he could have some company, maybe someone who knew him, who would smile at him and let him talk or be quiet as he chose. As Marya had back in Free Country. But—

His litany of woes and self-recrimination was halted by a startling sight. A strange movement above him caught his eye. He glanced up and gasped. "Blimey," Daniel exclaimed. "A blooming flying cat!"

He stood, his eyes tracking the bizarre crea- ture, and he noticed a startling detail—as if a flying cat wasn't startling enough. "The cat's fur is dry. It's not raining on the critter."

He let out a whooping laugh. "That's magic if I ever saw it! If that birdie-bat-cat is Timothy Hunter, then I didn't cause his death after all! He might have survived! Ooooh—I has to know for sure."

Daniel swung himself over the side of the roof and landed with a thud on the fire escape. "And maybe," he realized, his heart pounding as he clambered down the metal steps, "just maybe, he'll know where Marya is."

Chapter Three

Tim HOPED HE'D FIND Molly soon. He was getting tired. It took an awful lot of energy to keep his cat self quiet and happy by repelling the rain, and flying was hard work.

"The weight distribution is wrong," Tim complained as he struggled to avoid the top branches of a tree at the entrance to a park.

You should have listened to me. Cats stay on the ground.

"I get that, okay?" Tim worked to get his cat-bat-boy body above the treetops. "I see now why cats don't have wings. The back end is too heavy."

My back end is perfect.

"Hang on. I think I see her." Tim pumped his wings and fluttered toward a huge tree in the center of the park. Two girls sat beneath it. One girl was a little older than Tim, with long red hair and delicate features—Marya. The other girl was his age with thick dark hair, wearing jeans, a sweatshirt, and heavy work boots. That was Molly. The two girls huddled together, trying to keep dry under the massive tree branches.

"There she is!" Tim exclaimed. His cat eyes served him very well, picking out even the tiniest movements and creatures below him.

He came in for a landing, his cat self balking at having to put its paws on the squishy, muddy ground.

"Get a grip," Tim ordered. "You're a cat! An animal. You're supposed to be into dirt and stuff."

His cat nose sniffed. *You must be confusing me with those loathsome dog creatures.*

"Whatever." Tim crept toward Molly and Marya, anticipating the amazing moment when he would turn back into himself in front of them. That would be an impressive trick!

Not that he felt like he had to impress them— especially not Molly. But it would be cool to demonstrate something spectacular, now that he was getting a handle on this magic thing. Also, it would be nice to show Molly that magic could be more than demons and kidnapping and getting grounded.

First thing, though, he wanted to ditch the wings. They were so awkward, and he figured the girls would freak if a cat-bat hybrid started frolicking in front of them.

Once the wings vanished, Tim's cat self purred. *Much better. Now food?*

"Shh. They look serious," Tim observed. What was so important that Molly would sneak out of her house to see Marya in the middle of the night? He decided he'd listen for just a minute— not *really* eavesdrop—just to be sure he wasn't interrupting embarrassing girl talk.

"So what do you think I should do?" Molly was saying. "Should I tell Tim?"

Tim's pointy cat ears stood up. *Tell him what?*

"What's stopping you?" Marya asked. "You've never kept a secret from him before, have you?"

"Of course not," Molly said. "But this is so big. I want to tell him, but I'm afraid to. I don't know what he'll do."

"What do you mean? He's Tim. He'll do what's right."

Multiple emotions flooded through Tim. Shock that Molly was keeping something from him. Pride that Marya would assume he'd handle it well. Fear. Because Molly herself was afraid.

Molly let out an exasperated sigh and stood up. "Haven't you been listening?" she demanded. "Picture this little conversation." She posed as if she were talking to an invisible Tim.

"Oh, Tim, how sweet of you to bring me

chocolates. How did you know they were my favorites?" she gushed. "By the way, there's something I've been meaning to tell you. That dragon we met in the Demon Playland—that was you!" She smiled broadly, maniacally, as if she were thrilled by what she was saying. "Oh, yes, we had a lovely chat while you were out being all knightly," she said, her voice syrupy sweet. "He told me he—*you*—sold his memories to demons to get more and more power."

She tapped her chin with a finger as if she were trying to remember the conversation. "Oh, yes, and the Tim from the future told me he loved me soooooooo much that he made hundreds of copies of me. That's right! And not only that—oh joy—he kept me prisoner to be trained to become his perfect little wifey."

Tim was too shocked to move.

Marya started giggling and Molly glared at her. "I'm sorry," Marya said, trying to control her laughter. "I know it's really serious, but the way you tell it, with your faces and your voices, it's just so funny."

"Funny?" Molly repeated. "Was it funny when Daniel went nuts and almost hit you? No! You got upset and sad—and you don't even like Daniel like a boyfriend."

Molly's shoulders sagged. "Think of what it's

like for me," she said softly. "To know that Tim might grow up to be evil and want to change me into something wretched. That could be the future. For real."

How can this be happening? Tim said to himself. *How can she be saying those things?*

You're the one who insisted on coming here.

"I think I'm going to be sick," Tim murmured.

Grass helps. Eat some.

Tim felt as if his brain were going to explode. "Shut up! You don't understand."

I understand grass perfectly well.

"That's *me* Molly's talking about. Me!" His heart thudded under the cat fur. He couldn't believe what Molly was saying could be true, but he knew she wouldn't lie. He had to hear more, so he quieted the cat thoughts and tried to pay attention, despite his tormented feelings.

"I'm sorry," Marya said. She stood and put her arm around Molly's shoulders. "I know how terrible this is."

Molly nodded, and Tim could tell she wasn't actually mad at Marya. Just upset.

"I don't know which would be worse," Molly said. "To tell him or not to tell him. And should I break up with him because of something that only *might* happen?"

"Break up with me?" A lump formed in Tim's

furry throat and he was glad that cats couldn't cry.

"Might happen? You mean it's not definite?" Marya asked.

"The dragon told me that it was possible that he might not grow up to do those things," Molly said. "The future can be changed."

"Well, then that's good!" Marya said. "Right?"

Tim's tail flicked. "Yes! Right! The future can be changed! So let's change it."

"Right," Molly mumbled. "And Tim did promise me," she added, her face brightening a little. "He promised to never make deals with demons. That should make things okay."

"Yeah, sure." A throaty voice laughed near Tim. A tall woman stepped out of the bushes and approached the two girls. "And men always keep their promises. Especially ones they make at the tender age of thirteen."

The two girls gaped at the stranger, and so did Tim. She was pretty astonishing to look at. "Hot" might be a word some of the boys in his class would have used to describe her. She wore a strapless, skintight leather jumpsuit that emphasized her curves. Her thick black eyeliner made her green eyes look huge, and her long blond hair was pulled back in a ponytail. "Intense" was Tim's impression of her. She carried a birdcage, which made him wonder even more about who she was and what she was doing in the park in the rain. And why she decided to butt into Molly and Marya's conversation.

Tim crept closer. Both he and his cat self were curious about this stranger, though perhaps it was the bird in the cage that attracted the cat. Using his excellent cat vision he could see that Marya was intrigued by the woman and that Molly was wary. Tim trusted Molly's judgment.

"Hi!" Marya said. "I'm Marya, this is Molly."

The woman nodded. "Ladies," she greeted them with a smile. "Don't mean to interrupt your little gab session. I thought maybe you could benefit from the advice of someone older and perhaps wiser."

"Meaning you?" Molly gave the woman a slow once-over. "I don't think anyone wise would wear heels that high."

The woman laughed. "I like you. You're feisty."

"We were just talking about Molly's boyfriend," Marya explained.

Tim saw Molly's jaw tighten; he was sure she didn't want her personal life blathered to this woman. That wasn't her style.

"So I gathered," the woman said. "I take it he's a magician. Good, bad, or stupid?"

Molly put her hands on her hips. "What do you

mean, stupid?" she demanded. Then she shook her head. "Forget it. Come on, Marya, let's go."

"Awww, you don't want to break up the party just yet," the woman said. "After all, we still haven't solved your boyfriend problem." She put down the birdcage. "Let me see if I can do something about this weather, shall I?"

Tim stared as the woman threw her head back and lifted her arms up to the sky. Her lips were moving, but even with his enhanced cat hearing, he couldn't make out what she was saying. As the woman chanted softly, she began to glow, and Marya grabbed Molly's hand. The girls took a few stunned steps backward, their eyes never leaving the woman.

The glow spread out from the woman into the air around her. The farther it got from her, the less intense it became.

"She's using that energy to send the rain away from her," Tim murmured. He could do that to keep his cat body dry, but this woman was keeping the rain from falling on the whole park. "She packs a serious magic punch," he realized. Did that mean Molly and Marya were in danger? He didn't sense evil from her, but you never could tell.

Soon the woman stopped glowing. She lowered her arms and grinned at the girls. "Much

better. Moonlight's best for girl talk, don't you
think?"

She bent down and opened the birdcage. She
pulled the bird out and held it on her palm. "And
better for you, too," she told the bird. The bird
gazed into her eyes, then fluttered away, soaring
behind the leaves of a tall tree and disappearing.

As if stopping rain were the most normal
thing in the world, she sat cross-legged on the
grass. "Now, Ms. Molly, just between us sisters,
what's wrong with your guy?"

Molly gaped at her. "Who *are* you?"

The woman smirked. "I'm known as the Body
Artist. I'm the fairy-tale princess who ditches the
prince and saves herself, then conquers the neigh-
boring kingdom. I'm the answer to the questions
that don't get asked in those quizzes in *Seventeen*
and *Cosmo*. I don't hurt anyone, and I never let
anyone hurt me."

"How did you do that?" Marya asked. "Glow
and make it stop raining?"

"Ah, that's one of the first things a witch like
me learns. We're pretty hooked into natural sys-
tems: weather, plants, the body."

Molly's eyes narrowed. "So, are you good,
bad, or stupid?"

The woman laughed a deep, throaty laugh.
"Touché. Nothing gets by you, does it? Well, let's

just say I spend a lot of time in the gray areas of life. I live by a code, and I'm a moral and ethical being, but there are those who . . . don't like me. I don't truck with demons, and I don't like those who do."

That seemed to satisfy Molly. She sat beside the woman. "The grass is even dry!" she exclaimed with surprise.

"Never do anything partway, that's one of my mottoes."

Marya sat down, too, tucking her feet up under her dress. "Do you have others?"

The woman shrugged. "I just make them up as I go along."

"How much did you hear?" Molly asked.

"That your magic boyfriend may grow up to be a seriously bad bloke, and if he does, he'll take you down."

Her tough, no-frills summary of the situation made Molly bite her lip. Tim could see her blinking back tears, and it made him sick to know that he was the cause of her fear. Her potentially miserable future.

"I can't imagine Tim doing any of that stuff to me—ever. He's just too sweet, and he really likes me." Molly's voice was plaintive, but then her expression grew hard. "But I know other girls who've thought the same thing about their boyfriends and wound up getting hurt. Really hurt."

"Yeah . . ." Marya said softly. Tim knew she was thinking about Daniel. Daniel was crazy about Marya, but he had tried to hurt her anyway.

"I've thought about telling him everything that his maybe-someday-future self told me," Molly went on, "just telling him straight out. But he's already dealing with so much since the whole magic thing happened. And he felt terrible that those repulsive dino demons kidnapped me."

Molly sighed and pushed her dark hair away from her troubled face. "I've also thought about telling him that I can't see him anymore. But that's not what I want to do. I don't want to give up. Besides, it wouldn't be fair. He hasn't done anything bad yet. And maybe he never will."

That dragon must have been convincing, Tim realized. He was still having trouble understanding all the implications of what he was hearing. How could he believe that when he got older he'd do terrible things, including hurt Molly? But how could he *not* believe it? Molly wouldn't be so upset if she didn't believe it could be true. And if she was right, how could he live with himself?

"I think there's another reason you're so confused," said Marya. "You're scared that breaking up with Tim might be the very thing that will turn him crazy and mean."

Molly nodded, then pulled her knees up toward her chest. She wrapped her arms around her knees and rested her forehead on them, so that Tim could no longer see her face.

Marya turned to the Body Artist. "That's how it was with me and Daniel," she explained. "He was always nice to me. Until he realized I didn't want to be his girlfriend. Then he went all—"

Suddenly Daniel leaped out of the bushes. "I'm sorry, Marya!" he exclaimed.

"Daniel!" Marya gasped.

Tim's fur bristled and a low growl rumbled in his cat throat. Tim knew Daniel could be dangerous from experience; his cat self responded to the troubled boy on instinct.

"I love you, Marya," Daniel rushed on. "I'm sorry about the time I yelled at you and almost hit you. I wants to square things with you so's we can get back the way we used to be."

Molly was on her feet, and standing between Daniel and Marya. "Hey, back off, buddy."

Daniel ignored her and kept talking over her shoulder to Marya. "You got to forgive me, Marya. And take me back—or I'll kill myself," he said.

"But I can't take you back, Daniel," Marya replied. "You were never my boyfriend in the first place. I was never your girlfriend. That's the part you don't understand."

Tim saw anger flash across the boy's face. "If you don't agree to love me I'll—I'll jump in the river and drown myself dead."

"Get over yourself," Molly said. "Why can't you listen?"

"Why can't you mind your own business?" Daniel responded.

Tim moved closer, hunkering down, preparing to spring. Just then the Body Artist reached over and grabbed him by the scruff of his neck. He was too surprised to even meow.

"Hey," she whispered into his cat ears as she stroked the top of his head. "What's the hurry? He's not going to do anything until he's milked this melodramatic scene for all it's worth."

She held the cat so that they faced each other, eye to eye.

"Cat. I name you Cat," she said. "Nose to tail. Whiskers to paws. Cat. Claws in. Mind blank. Mouth shut. Cat."

It all happened so fast. Tim couldn't tear his eyes away from her clear green gaze. He felt himself go slightly woozy. He blinked and stared at the scene in front of him. *Girls*, he thought. *And a boy. No food?*

"Hah!" The Body Artist smirked. "You've got a lot to learn, kiddo. You have to take precautions when you're shape-walking, Tim-Cat. You might find yourself named and shape bound. Like this."

She quickly shoved him into the birdcage and locked the little door. "Now you just park your tail, kitty. I'll be right with you. I need to make some changes in this little drama in front of us."

"This is between me and Marya," Daniel hissed at Molly.

"It's going to be between you and my fists if you don't quit bugging us," Molly said.

Daniel hung his head and his whole body drooped. "I mess up everything."

Marya put her hand on Molly's arm. "He does seem different. More sad and less . . ."

"Homicidal?" Molly finished for her.

"I guess. I don't think he'd harm us."

"I don't trust him," Molly grumbled.

"That's because he's not trustworthy yet," the Body Artist said. "How can he be? He's a walking wound."

"What?" Daniel demanded, fire flashing in his eyes again. "Someone else 'as an opinion now?"

"Daniel!" the Body Artist declared. She planted her feet far apart and stared at him. Light glowed around her, and all three kids stared at her. Molly shielded her eyes from the blinding glare.

Shafts of white light shot out of the woman

straight into Daniel, lifting him off the ground.

"Put me down!" he shouted. "Leave me be! I never meant to hurt nobody."

"What are you doing to him?" Molly yelled.

The Body Artist lowered Daniel to the ground. "Oh, it stings," he moaned, writhing on all fours. "It stings."

"Daniel!" Marya cried. "Don't hurt him, please!"

Daniel shuddered and contorted, letting out an agonizing howl, which turned into a yowl, which turned into a whimper.

Molly and Marya gaped at the astounding sight: Daniel was gone, and there was now an adorable puppy in his place.

"What did you do to him?" Marya asked. She knelt down and the puppy put his little paws on her knees. He gave her chin a lick, and Marya giggled.

"I gave him a body to match his needs," the Body Artist explained.

Marya stood and threw a stick for the puppy to fetch. He bounded off after it, tail wagging.

"You made him a dog? Are you nuts?" Molly shrieked. "That's just cruel."

"Is it? How so?" the Body Artist challenged. "He's getting all the benefits of a first-rate reincarnation and he didn't even have to die first.

What's cruel about that?"

The puppy who had once been Daniel returned, carrying the stick proudly. Marya took it from him. "Good little doggie," she crooned, petting him. The dog's tail wagged furiously.

"Look at them, Molly," the Body Artist continued. "That puppy is going to get all the love and attention Daniel has always craved, that he's been denied his whole life."

Now Marya ran in little circles, the puppy chasing her gleefully.

"The lack of that affection is what turned Daniel bitter and sour," the Body Artist said. "Once he experiences enough love to fill the void in him, he'll be safe to be human again."

Molly rolled her eyes. "I still say it's sick. Now he can follow Marya around all the time, and she'll love it. But what do you think will happen when he's human again?" Molly shook her head. "I want you to keep your perky little nose out of my love life! I can't believe I told you all that stuff about me and Tim. If turning Daniel into a puppy is your idea of a solution, I'd hate to think of the advice you might have for me!"

The Body Artist shrugged. "Okay. I get it, girlfriend. You go your way, and I'll go mine."

The woman picked up the cage with the cat inside it and walked away. The cat enjoyed the swaying rhythm as she carried him, but for some reason he couldn't explain, his tail flicked anxiously as the two girls got smaller and smaller behind him.

"That's quite a girl you've got there, Tim-Cat," the Body Artist commented. "Maybe you'll deserve her one of these days."

Chapter Four

THE BODY ARTIST CARRIED the cat-boy-magician through the dark streets of London. The rain had stopped, which pleased her. It meant she didn't have to bother using her energy to keep herself dry.

She passed several rough bars and bohemian cafés; small locked-up, gated shops; and a few furtive, dark-clothed people. She didn't want anyone to notice her, so no one did, despite her eye-grabbing appearance.

She came to a seedy street, turned the corner, and unlocked the door to a darkened store. The words "Circe's Tattooing, Piercing, and Other Alterations" were etched on the glass door.

She flicked on the lights and placed the cage holding the cat on a stainless steel table. "So, tell me, Tim-Cat, how long have you been doing the shape-walk?"

The cat yawned and rolled over.

"Tim-Cat? Hello?" She slipped a finger with a long violet-painted nail between the bars of the cage and scratched the cat under the chin. "I'm talking to you."

The cat pressed its face against her finger and purred.

"Oh, I forgot," the Body Artist said. "You're still charmed. Silly me. Sorry about that. I hate one-sided conversations."

She bent down so that she could look the cat in the eyes. "Cat, hear your name. Cat, wake. Sharp of eye. Keen of ear. Clear of mind. Wake."

The cat gave a small shake of its head and suddenly seemed more alert.

"That's better," the Body Artist declared. "Maybe now we can have a nice little chat."

Cat-Tim gazed through the bars of a cage. "Mrrrrow!" it complained. *I want to go outside.*

"Huh?" Tim's thoughts were all mixed up, and he felt very quiet inside his groggy brain. The cat's thoughts were stronger and louder.

Outside! Cat-Tim insisted. *Outside right now.*

Tim's eyes finally took in his surroundings. The bars, the strange place. The intense woman from the park. "That doesn't seem to be an option at the moment," Tim explained to the cat.

But there are pigeons to chase outside.

"We're in a cage, you dweeb," Tim said, "or hadn't you noticed? Sheesh!"

The cat sat up on its hind legs and placed its front paws on the bars, straining to get to the pigeons perched on the windowsill outside. *But I see pigeons to play with. Don't you?*

"Tim-Cat, do you mind?" the Body Artist said. "I'd like to speak to you. Now then, are you taking any medications? Have any allergies? Meow once for yes, twice for no."

Look! The fat pigeon just flew into the wall! How silly.

The Body Artist cocked her head and looked at him. "Tim-Cat? What is the matter with you?"

I want to go outside, Cat-Tim insisted.

"Outside," Tim repeated. If it was possible for a brain to yawn, Tim's did. "Outside."

"You want to go—?" The Body Artist let out a hooting laugh. "Snap out of it, Tim! You're getting all tangled up in body thoughts. You're letting the cat part take over."

She flicked her violet nails on the bars of the cage, then gave it a shake. "Yoo-hoo! Wake up, Tim!"

The movement jolted Tim. "What?" he asked. He gazed around the room. "What's going on?"

We're going to go see pigeons, Cat-Tim replied.

"Shut up about the bloody pigeons," Tim

ordered. "I don't want to think about stupid birds.
I want to think about getting out of here!"

"Listen up, Timmy-Kitty," the Body Artist
said. "Here's your problem. You've hooked your
consciousness straight into your body's autonomic
nervous system. That's wrong."

"I'll tell you what's wrong," Tim snapped.
"Being a cat is wrong. Being here is . . ." His eyes
wandered around the room. He spotted a collec-
tion of terrifying-looking tools and stuff he imagined lunatic doctors used in crazy science
experiments. "Being here is definitely wrong."

"Hey, who told you to turn yourself into a cat
in the first place?" the Body Artist countered.
"Shape work is like driving. You don't crawl inside
the motor to make the car go, you sit behind the
wheel." She gave him another look. "Oh wait.
That example won't work for you—you're too
young to drive. You probably don't even shave
yet."

She laughed sharply and gave him a smirk.
The woman reminded Tim of someone, but Cat-
Tim was taking up too much space in his brain for
him to remember who. He had noticed it in the
park, too, some familiar quality, particularly in the
way she had talked to Marya and Molly.

"It would be terribly unfair of me to read you
as though you were a grown man, but I suppose

I've got to," she said, tapping her purple finger-nails on the cage. "You're not likely to give me another chance to open you up after this. And you're simply too powerful to be trusted."

"Open me up? What do you mean?" That didn't sound promising to Tim. He didn't like the fact that she could obviously read his thoughts—both his and the cat's. How much more "reading" did she have in mind?

But if•the Body Artist heard his questions, she ignored them. She began clearing off a nearby table. "Do you know how long I had to study shap-ing before I could borrow a cat's body? But you—you did it on the spur of the moment, didn't you?"

"It seemed like a good idea at the time," Tim responded.

I don't remember, Cat-Tim said.

The Body Artist blinked and looked puzzled. Then her eyes narrowed with wary suspicion. "Hang on," she murmured. She stood in front of the cage, staring hard at Tim.

Tim felt a strange sensation in his head, almost a tickle. A warm wave ran through him, and then everything was normal again.

The Body Artist gasped and stepped away from him. "I don't believe it," she exclaimed. "You didn't *borrow* that body. You *made* it. From nothing. How much power do you have?"

Tim's cat senses could feel the fear in her. It made him afraid, too, because her fear was mixed with anger.

She paced the room. "So the rumors about your power are true. And your girl, Molly, has good reason to be afraid. You have all the potential to become exactly what she described in your future."

She got herself under control and approached the cage again. "I'm not so concerned anymore about treating you like a grown man. I should treat you like a sworn enemy, until I know otherwise. I've never seen this kind of power."

"But—"

"Nighty-night, now, kitty. Named Cat. Bound Cat. Cat-Tim. Sleep. Sleep now."

Tim couldn't fight it. His eyes closed and all of his muscles went limp.

"Good kitty," the Body Artist said.

It sounded a lot like a purr.

Chapter Five

THE BODY ARTIST LAID the sleeping cat on her stainless steel table. "This ability of yours must have some inner creature driving it," she murmured. "Or, given your age, some force from the outside guiding it." She shook her head. "How did you convince that sweet little girl you're a whole human person? Molly seemed sharp as a tack. And yet . . ." She bit her lip, thinking about the conversation in the park. "I suppose this is precisely why she's feeling so tormented. The contradiction between what she knows and how you appear."

The Body Artist gazed down at the shaped cat, trying to guess what kind of person lay inside it. "What are you?" she asked the sleeping creature. "Some instrument created by the evil ones? A demon god? Well, I'll find out now."

She held out her hand and a shimmering,

surgical tool appeared in it. It was insubstantial, made of energy only, but she could grip it with sureness.

She positioned her tool above the cat. "Now, let's see what we can find here."

Using the magical implement, she cut open the cat body, reached inside, and lifted a ghostly form from it. This was Tim's inner self—complete with T-shirt and glasses.

Not a bad self-image, she thought, holding it up to inspect it. *And it's suffused with light energy—so if he's to align with the dark forces, it hasn't happened yet.*

Still, she was certain that the potential for evil had to be there. She just had to keep looking for it.

She pulled Tim's ghostly self completely from the cat shape, and as she did, the cat form rippled, then turned back into the boy it had once been. "Bye-bye, kitty," the Body Artist said. She gave Tim's regular body a quick appraisal, then laid his ghostly one on another table to really start her work.

"Seam ripper," she commanded, and a tool leaped into her hand. She glanced at it. "Not you. The one with the insulated grip."

She began cutting into Tim's ethereal body. "Huh. That's odd. No resistance." As she continued to work, she grew more and more puzzled.

I don't understand. I should have hit some darkness by now if he's going to grow up to become the monster Molly described. Something must be wrong. She put down her tool and drummed her long fingernails on the steel table. *Well, it could be a case of inner beastliness, I suppose. At least that's fixable.*

"Heart seeker," she ordered. A grisly-looking device materialized in the air in front of her. "Don't open the heart. At least not yet," she instructed. "Don't even scratch it. I just want to get a good look. Cut me a window."

The device did its work. It hovered a few inches from Tim's floating ethereal body, and as Tim's heart was revealed, the Body Artist sank to the floor, bathed in the light streaming from the boy.

Timothy Hunter felt cold. He opened his eyes and blinked a few times, trying to piece things together. His glasses were missing, so things were a bit blurry, as was his brain. He rubbed his eyes and noticed something—something important.

"Hands," he declared thickly. "I've got hands again."

He rolled over and spotted the blond woman

from the park sitting on a chair facing him. "You!"
he exclaimed. "Who are you? And what did you do
to me?"

She stared at him with enormous green eyes.

"Uh, miss? Are you okay?" Tim asked nervously.

"You're a boy," she murmured. "Just a boy."

"Well, I could have told you that," Tim grumbled. "Saved you a whole lot of trouble."

"You don't understand," the woman said.

"What's to understand? I understand you put
me in a cage!" As Tim sat up, he made the startling discovery that he wasn't wearing his clothes.
When—and how did that *happen?*

"Did you put me in a towel?" He felt himself
flush, and he couldn't decide if he was more
humiliated by the fact that she'd seen him without
his clothes or that his voice squeaked when he
yelled at her.

The woman's expression changed from
awestruck to amused. "Stop blushing," she said.
She stood and stretched, working her muscles as
if she'd been sitting there for a while. "I kept my
eyes closed the entire time."

"You did?"

"Well, no, but you don't need to be embar-
rassed. I'm a professional."

"Oh great," Tim scoffed, clutching the edge of the towel tightly. "That makes everything all better. A professional *what*?"

"Body artist." She waved a hand at the posters of heavily tattooed people behind her.

Tim didn't get what tattoos had to do with the current situation—or the magic he had seen her perform in the park. "I don't see anything artistic about hypnotizing people while they're cats," he argued. "Or locking them up in birdcages or taking their clothes."

"I didn't take your clothes," the Body Artist countered with a grin. "You didn't bring them with you on your little cat-capade."

Tim opened his mouth, then shut it again. She had him there. His jeans, his T-shirt, his sneakers, and his glasses must all still be at the fence behind Molly's house where he had worked the transformation. "Whatever. There's still no excuse for—"

The Body Artist interrupted him. "You heard what Molly said in the park. She found out that you might grow up to be someone who would do terrible things. Not just to her but also to the world. I brought you here to stop that from happening."

Tim stared at her. "Is that possible?"

She gave a rueful laugh. "Well, the problem is that all my theories were wrong. I'm a pretty decent witch, but you are one unique individual. So the technique I'd planned to use won't work."

"Why?"

"Several reasons." The Body Artist sat back in the chair and placed her feet up on one of the tables, crossing one booted ankle over the other. "For one, I may have dubious scruples, but I do have a code. I'd never alter a nondemon without his consent."

Her posture made Tim realize who she reminded him of: John Constantine. John had been one of the trench-coated strangers who had first introduced Tim to the world of magic. Tim had liked John a lot, and this woman's tough demeanor, gray-area mentality, and general arrogance were a lot like John's.

"When I discovered you weren't innately evil," she continued, "I thought maybe it was an inner animal problem."

"Huh?" Tim's eyebrows rose.

"Lots of people have some kind of animal inside," the Body Artist explained. "Don't ask me why. For most, it's part of their soul or heart, and it doesn't have to be bad. But in others, their beasts have consumed their humanity—crept up on it while it wasn't looking and eaten it, making them dangerous. I thought that if I could find your beast, I could force you to face it. And tame it."

"What would have happened if I wasn't tamable?"

"I would have pulled out your fangs or declawed you," the Body Artist replied. "But it doesn't matter. There's no animal in you."

Tim's heart sank. "So that evil future me might still happen." _And Molly is still in danger._

"What you will become is based on the choices that you make and on the ways in which you use your magic," the Body Artist told him. "And since you have no inner evil, I can't alter any aspect of you without your consent."

She sighed a long, frustrated sigh. "So look around the shop, find yourself something to wear, and I'll give you directions home. And cab fare if you need it."

"Isn't there _something_ you can do? To make sure I never hurt Molly?" Tim asked.

"Any number of things," the woman said flatly. "None of them pleasant."

"Then do it," Tim declared. "I consent. As long as I get to stay alive, that is, and stay myself. Do whatever magic you have to do to keep her safe from me."

The Body Artist's eyebrows rose. "Are you sure?"

"Am I sure that I want some morally ambiguous

witch to fiddle with me magically? No. Am I sure I'd rather die than hurt Molly? Yes. Only make sure it doesn't go *that* far, okay?" he added hastily.

"It's not easy," the Body Artist warned. "It's painful, and the pain continues."

"Why am I not surprised?" Tim commented.

"Just giving you full disclosure."

Tim nodded. "I've decided."

The woman gave him an admiring smile. "You're braver than I thought. You just might be good enough for Molly after all."

Chapter Six

I DON'T FEEL ANY different, Tim thought. *Well, other than very conspicuous.*

He glanced down at the clothing the Body Artist had given him to wear home. Environmentally correct fake-leather pants, a black T-shirt held together with safety pins, and pointy ankle boots.

"Someone should tell her that punk is seriously over," Tim said. Although he certainly didn't want to volunteer for the position of bursting her fashion bubble.

He wished he had thought to snag a pair of sunglasses. He blinked against the bright sunlight. He'd been out all night again. "Oh, great," he muttered. He was going to catch it from his dad for sure. He let out a sigh and shrugged. There was nothing he could do about it now.

She turned out to be pretty cool, Tim decided,

thinking about the Body Artist as he made his way to the Soho tube station. There was nothing fake about her—despite her theatrical makeup and costume-like clothing. She called things as she saw them, whether she thought you'd agree with her or not, or would like what you were hearing. Tim respected that. It was a far cry better than the grown-ups who treated people his age like babies, or pretended everything was so nicey-nice all the time. Rough honesty was her style, and Tim thought maybe he'd try to make it his style, too.

But how honest are you really being? he asked himself. *You eavesdropped on Molly, which was bad enough. Then you went and had the Body Artist alter you to prevent harming Molly any other way because you don't trust yourself. So in a way, you're now kind of a fake you.*

He tugged the neck of his borrowed shirt away from his body and tried to see the tattoos the Body Artist had inked onto his chest. There they were: a vicious-looking scorpion emblazoned above an oversized butterfly. All in vivid—and painful—color.

"There's so much power in you," the Body Artist had warned. "I have to use a two-pronged approach. These days it's all about specialization anyway."

She hadn't been kidding. Getting tattooed seri-

ously hurt. Tim wasn't sure if the pain was so intense because the tattoos were magical talismans or if all tattooing was a white-knuckle, teeth-gritting, howl-at-the-moon kind of experience. It had taken a while, but by the time he'd left the Body Artist's place, his body felt like his own again, and his nerve endings no longer felt like they were on fire.

At least I can come clean about it all when I see Molly, he told himself. *I'll feel a lot better after we talk this whole thing through.* He paid his fare with the coins the Body Artist had given him, and dashed onto a train.

The rocking movement of the train nearly put him to sleep. It had been a long, rough night. He'd expended a lot of energy being a cat. Then he'd been up all night dealing with the problem of his evil future. He looked forward to taking a long nap once he got home. That was one thing he could do while he was grounded.

Tim emerged above ground again and trudged toward his flat. He stopped himself. "No," he declared. *I'll see Molly first thing. Before I'm trapped in my house again, I'll tell her that she has nothing to worry about—I can't do magic anymore.*

He touched the tattoos on his chest, frowning. *At least, I don't think I can.* He stopped walking. *Maybe I should do a little test, just to be sure.*

He ducked into an alley. "Okay, what magic should I do?" He scanned the deserted alley. Without his glasses, it was a bit blurry. "Something simple." He bit his lip, deciding. His gaze landed on some dented garbage cans. "That'll do."

He stood in front of the garbage cans. He held his hands out toward them. He focused on the lids, intending to do nothing fancier than switching them. *Concentrate*, he told himself, letting his mind clear, as he always did before making magic, preparing to fill it back up again with images, intention, and will.

The familiar energy began to make his arms tingle, but then a searing pain shot through his chest. Tim collapsed to the ground, breaking his magical link to the garbage cans. The moment the magic was released, the pain stopped.

Tim lay on the filthy pavement, panting. His chest felt as if it had been burned from the inside out, while a million hot needles stung his skin.

"I guess these tattoos mean business," he moaned. They'd keep him from using magic for sure. He didn't want to experience that kind of pain again.

He slowly rolled over onto his knees and stood up. Last night's rain had left big puddles, so now his fake-leather jeans had big wet patches on the knees. He wiped his muddy, damp palms on the

T-shirt, hoping the Body Artist wasn't expecting him to return the borrowed clothing.

Oh, man. That was just level one magic, Tim realized. *The pain is probably even worse if I do something requiring more power.*

He made his way back to the street, feeling a strange mixture of emotions. He was relieved that he could honestly tell Molly that she had nothing to fear from his magic. Yet he felt sad, too. As if he'd lost something—something important.

"Forget magic," he told himself. "What's it done for you besides get you into a whole lot of trouble?"

He arrived at Molly's, and found the pile of his clothes and glasses just where he had left them when he'd turned into a cat the night before. He bundled up the clothes, and slipped on the glasses, then stood in front of Molly's door trying to figure out what to do.

"Maybe this wasn't such a hot idea," he muttered. He glanced down at his borrowed—and now damp and dirty—outfit. "Especially dressed like this."

Just as he was turning to go, the front door opened. One of Molly's older cousins, the tall one called Bridget, charged out of the house. There were always relatives coming and going at Molly's. Bridget skidded to a stop when she saw Tim.

"What are you doing here?" she demanded.

"Can you give Molly a message for me?" he asked.

Bridget grabbed his arm and yanked him into the alley. She looked down at him. "Unlikely. You're public enemy number one around here, remember?"

Tim's shoulders slumped. "I know, I know, but I swear, we didn't do anything wrong."

Bridget's expression softened. "I believe you, but that doesn't really mean anything. I could get into trouble just speaking to you."

"Then why are you?" Tim asked. "You could have run back into the house and ratted me out."

"I guess I feel sorry for you," Bridget admitted. "Besides, I don't have to protect you from Molly. She's not here."

"Where is she?" This was good news! Maybe Tim would be able to see Molly after all! "Is she at the library? The Swan Dance School?"

Bridget shook her head. "I mean she's *really* not here. Her parents sent her off to the country to stay at her Gran's."

"Wh-what?" Tim stammered.

"Yeah, they're even thinking of taking her out of school altogether, just to get her away from you," Bridget confided. "They think you're a bad influence." Her eyes traveled from his pointy boots to his safety-pinned T-shirt. "Can't say I blame them."

He stared at Bridget, trying to process what she was telling him. Molly was gone—possibly forever? *What was the point of getting these stupid tattoos if we can't even be together?*

Tim's heart began to pound hard, and an intense burning spread across his chest. He was afraid to say anything in case speaking made the pain worse. Besides, what was there to say? So he just turned and dashed away.

"Tim? Are you okay?" Bridget called after him.

Tim clutched his T-shirt, pulling it away from his burning chest. The more upset he got the worse the stinging became. He ducked down a side street and slammed his back up against a wall, needing the bricks to hold him up. He took in great gulps of air trying to force himself to calm down.

"I'm not allowed to feel anything either?" he gasped. "Is that the deal here? No magic and no emotions?"

Pain made him sweat, stinging his eyes. He shut them tight behind his glasses. "Okay!" he shouted, smacking the wall behind him. "You win! I won't feel anything ever again! I'll stop being natural right now! Are you satisfied?"

To distract himself, he counted as he inhaled

and exhaled. His chest rose and sank with the deep breaths he was taking, and gradually the waves of pain subsided.

Exhausted, he slumped over, putting his hands on his bent knees, trying to recover. His heart slowed back to its normal pace, and he could think more clearly.

I guess it was still a good idea to get these tattoos, he assured himself as he got up and headed to his house. *There is still all of humanity to worry about if I become evil. My magic doesn't just affect Molly.*

Tim arrived back home, drained, damp, and miserable. He didn't even try sneaking back in; he just stuck his key in the lock. Before he could turn it, though, the door swung wide open, yanking the key out of Tim's hand.

"I've been waiting for you," Mr. Hunter fumed.

He must have been waiting on the other side of the door, Tim realized. *Was he patrolling the front hall all night?*

"Where have you been?" Mr. Hunter demanded.

"I— I was out," Tim said feebly. He knew it sounded stupid but at least it was true.

Mr. Hunter glared at Tim. "I gathered that. If you're going to stay out all night, with no consideration for me and my worries, then why don't you just stay out for good!"

Without another word, Mr. Hunter slammed the door in Tim's face.

Tim's mouth dropped open, and he blinked a few times. "Wh-what?" he stammered at the closed door. *Did my dad just kick me out?*

He stumbled away from the door, aware of the burning in his chest, and then ran as hard as he could down the street. He had no idea where he was going, he just knew he had to get there fast.

Mr. Hunter stood inside the house with his back to the door, counting to ten. When he reached ten he was still furious, so he counted to ten again. He needed to get a grip on his emotions before talking to Tim. He was worried about the lad; something must have happened recently that had sent the boy into a sort of tailspin. He'd always been a bit dreamy, but Tim seemed so lost, so distracted these days.

I just pray it isn't drugs. Mr. Hunter was fairly certain drugs were not the cause of Tim's erratic behavior. Drugs wouldn't have made Tim ask about his parentage. *Though I suppose the answer—that I am not his biological father—could have sent him down that self-destructive path.*

Mr. Hunter was convinced that Tim had always been too self-possessed, even as a child, to turn to something like drugs. *Tim's not one to give in to peer pressure*, Mr. Hunter thought. *And the boy has always seemed far too interested in reality for drugs to appeal to him. In fact*, Mr. Hunter thought uncomfortably, *Tim's always giving me a hard time about being lost in my own dreamworld of telly and the car in the parking lot*. No, this was not a drug problem. This was something else. And Mr. Hunter wanted to help Tim through it, if only he could figure out how.

Much calmer, he felt ready to have a talk with the lad. He reopened the door, and his heart sank. The street was empty.

"Tim!" he shouted in one direction, then another. "Tim!" he called again. It was no use. The boy was gone.

I hope that I haven't driven him off for good. Mr. Hunter knew he could never forgive himself if he had.

Chapter Seven

TIM RAN AND RAN, and then ran some more. He had no destination in mind, except maybe oblivion. Just run right into nothingness, to a place where he was no one, where he could start over, where Molly wasn't gone, where he didn't disappoint his dad or make people angry. Run and run and run till his brain emptied out.

His breath came hard, but he didn't stop. Where could he go? Where could he rest? There was no respite for him anywhere. Not since bloody magic wrecked his life.

He took a corner fast, and wished for his skateboard. The speed would be even greater, the breeze stronger, the sense of movement more intense. He pounded his feet on the pavement, bounced off curbs, leaped over puddles.

I should have gone out for track after all, he thought. The exertion was beginning to get to him, though. No sleep, no food since breakfast yesterday, plus the pain he'd endured at the hands of the Body Artist.

She had helped him; maybe he should go there. But he wasn't sure what she could do for him now.

Tim dashed into the street, when a car suddenly spun around a corner and barreled straight toward him. Without even thinking Tim flung out his hand and sent the car swerving around him.

"Prat," Tim muttered as he headed for an alley. He glanced back. The car was still careening through the streets at a ridiculous speed, never even slowing down. "Jerk!" he shouted.

Tim doubled over in agony. The tattoos! "Arrgh!" Tim clutched his rumpled clothes to his chest and sank to the ground. Dropping the jeans and T-shirt he'd retrieved at Molly's, he crouched on all fours, trying to survive the onslaught of pain.

"Stop it!" he begged. "All right! I was angry! And I used magic! But that driver deserved it. He was a menace to society!"

The tattoos stung harder, like a million needles. "He didn't brake," Tim said, gasping, still protesting the unfairness of it all. "He didn't even honk. I could have been—" The pain cut off his ability to speak.

Sweat streamed down his face, his back. "All right," he choked out. "I get it. No more big emotions. No more magic. No more, please."

The pain subsided; and exhausted, Tim crawled over to the wall and sat, leaning against the back door of a shop. He looked down his shirt and addressed his tattoos.

"You've got a strange way of trying to save me from myself," he said. "That is what you're supposed to be doing, right? I mean, you could have killed me when I fell over like that. What if I'd banged my head on the curb? Or let that car hit me?"

He sighed and sat staring for a while, with no idea of how much time might be passing. He felt empty. Like he'd gone blank. It was a comforting feeling.

"Timothy Hunter, is that you?"

Tim glanced over at the familiar voice. Marya stood at the entrance to the alley, holding the little puppy that had once been Daniel on a leash.

Instead of being relieved to have found a friend, seeing Marya just made Tim feel worse. Partly because she and Molly were so tight, and Tim wasn't in any way prepared to talk about any of *that*. It was also because Marya was part of this whole magical life causing him so much trouble. He had saved her world, Free Country, and then she had stayed on in London. She was human, sure, but she had not lived a normal human life. And it seriously did not help that Daniel was with her—boys turned into puppies and girls from magical realms. It was just too much to take in.

Marya came over and knelt beside him, Daniel following with his tail wagging. Tim could see why Daniel liked her so much. She was very pretty, but it was also because there was something gentle about her. Maybe it was because she had spent so much time in Free Country, where kids were never supposed to worry about anyone ever hurting them. Bad magic had nearly destroyed that sanctuary—the way magic seemed to screw up everything.

"Tim," she said again, tucking her long red hair behind her ears. "Are you okay? You look terrible."

"I'm not surprised," he admitted. "I feel pretty bad." The puppy stuck his nose in Tim's face and sniffed. Tim gently pushed the dog away. "Quit it, Daniel. The last thing I need is chimney-sweep dog slobber all over me."

Marya tugged on the puppy's leash, and it bounded back to sit at her feet. *On* her feet, actually.

"Listen, Marya," Tim said. "Nothing personal, but can you kind of go away?"

"What?" She shook her head. "No. If you feel bad, you shouldn't be alone."

"Actually, being alone is exactly what I need right now." Tim held up a hand to keep her from protesting. "Really. I'm too tired, and too confused, to talk right now. Okay?"

"We don't have to talk. We can just sit. Daniel and I used to do that." She smiled. "We do a lot more of it now." She cuddled the dog to her. He licked her nose, making her giggle.

This is too weird for me. Watching Marya and Daniel was freaking out Tim even more, even though both dog and girl seemed quite pleased with the arrangement.

"I mean it, Marya. Please. If you really are my friend, you'll go away. I just have to—sort things out. I won't be able to do that if you're here."

Marya's face was still worried and uncertain. Tim had to come up with something that would make her leave him there, alone.

"I'll feel too self-conscious with you sitting here and us not talking," Tim said. "And I'm just not up to talking."

That's good, he thought. *She can't argue with this excuse, especially since it's also true.*

Marya bit her lip. "Well . . ." She stood back up, cradling the puppy in her arms. "If you're sure . . ." Her voice trailed off, still unconvinced.

Tim nodded. "I'm sure. See you."

"Okay. See you." Marya walked back out of the alley, giving Tim a last long look, and then vanished.

Tim slumped. The exchange with Marya had taken a lot out of him, given his already high level of exhaustion. He bundled up his spare clothes and rested his head on them. *No food and no sleep and serious emotional turmoil can sure tucker you out.* Soon, he fell into a dreamless, fitful sleep.

A strange nightmarish creature, a creature made of odds and ends, of castoffs, and of garbage, blocked the entrance to the alley.

The Wobbly.

A creation of Tim's childhood imagination, made real by Tim's magic, the Wobbly was a creature who got rid of the unwanted, the discarded. The Wobbly had a skull-like face that resembled another scavenger, the vulture. It hovered a few feet above the ground, its talons scraping the pavement. If Tim had been awake he would have seen that the Wobbly had grown since their last encounter.

"Are you now one of the useless, Opener?" the Wobbly rasped. It made its way toward Tim. "If so, I will find use for you. I will . . . *recycle*, as you once told me was the new way."

The Wobbly loomed over the boy's prone form. "Yes, I see how it is with you, Opener. You will be good to use to feather my nest. In bits and pieces. You have thrown yourself away, and now I take you for recycling." It reached out a skeletal claw toward the sleeping boy.

"No." A voice stopped the Wobbly. "Not thrown away." A thick man rummaging through a nearby garbage can stood up. He, too, was something of a scavenger. His battered khaki jacket had had many previous owners. The newspapers he wrapped around his feet as shoes had been found on the park bench near where he slept.

The man turned to face the Wobbly and scratched his full salt-and-pepper beard. "You have misunderstood his situation. The boy has simply lost himself. He has not discarded himself."

"Ahhhhh?" The Wobbly sounded puzzled. "There is a difference?"

"Oh, yes, my friend. A big difference."

"He is not for taking?" the Wobbly asked.

"Not by you, Mr. Birdhead." The thick man bent down and lifted Tim in his powerful arms. The boy was so deeply asleep he merely mumbled and flopped over the man's shoulder. "The boy will come with me." He grabbed the clothes Tim had been using as a pillow, picked up the large garbage bag filled with his own belongings, and strode out of the alley.

Chapter Eight

TIM FELT VERY GROGGY. He'd been deeply
asleep for some time; his muscles were stiff and
he didn't want to think about what his breath
must be like. He rubbed his face, trying to get his
brain back into gear. "Man, what truck hit me?" he
muttered.

"The reality truck, perhaps? I hear it's a
doozy."

Tim sat up, instantly alert. The room was
dark, and it took a few minutes for Tim to get his
bearings. A stocky old man sat on the floor across
from him.

"Kenny?" Tim recognized the man. He was an
old homeless guy that Tim's real father, Tamlin,
had introduced him to. In fact, Tim's very first
magic was keeping snow from falling on Kenny
last winter. That seemed a long time ago now.

"In the flesh," the man replied. "Glad you

finally woke. I was beginning to worry that the Wobbly had been right."

"You've seen the Wobbly?" Even though Tim, as the Opener, had created the Wobbly, the peculiar creature made him nervous. He was also surprised the Wobbly had been visible to Kenny; usually these creatures couldn't be seen by too many others besides Tim.

"I've seen him, indeed. The Wobbly thought you'd thrown yourself away. You haven't, have you? I'd hate to have been made a liar by a young sprout like you."

"Not that I know of," Tim replied, "though the idea is tempting." Tim swung his legs over the side of the bed and took in the room: the narrow bed with the thin mattress, the peeling paint, the obvious lack of a bathroom or kitchen. "Where am I?"

"The Full Moon hotel," Kenny replied. "It has a no-stars rating, but the terms are reasonable."

"Is this where you live?" Tim asked. He had thought Kenny was homeless. At least, he had been back in the winter.

"Me? Stay in one place? Indoors? Never." The man laughed a wheezing laugh.

"But if you could find a place for me, why don't you find a place for yourself?" Tim asked.

The man shuddered. "I was once confined. I didn't like it."

"Were you—Were you in prison?" Tim asked, hoping he wasn't being too personal.

"Oh no. Nothing like that. Well, actually something like that, in how I felt. I prefer open spaces. There is always some light under the open sky. I don't much care for the dark."

"Oh," Tim said, even though he didn't really understand.

"This place is run by old friends," Kenny said. "You are safe here."

Tim nodded, then yawned. "'Scuse me," he said. "I don't know why I'm so tired."

"Fatigue is the constant companion of one at war."

"At war?" Tim repeated. "I'm not fighting any war."

"Aren't you?" Kenny asked. "You bear the signs."

Tim wanted to ask Kenny what he meant, but all he could think of was sleep. He couldn't keep his eyes open, so finally he quit fighting it. He drifted off quickly.

The moment he was sure that Tim was asleep, Kenny lit a candle and placed it in the center of the room. "Even in your sleep you feel the battle," he told the sleeping boy. "Together perhaps we can find a way to end it."

Kenny crouched in the corner of the small

hotel room and waited. He knew he'd see the same fight he'd seen the past two nights since he'd taken in Tamlin's son. The boy had Tamlin's fire, that was sure. But he was also an innocent, and troubled, and he had lost the one man who could have guided him well. It was up to Kenny, as Tamlin's friend, to help the boy back onto the path. If the boy was willing to be helped, that is.

Tim's T-shirt fluttered. Two creatures, insubstantial, two-dimensional, crept out from under the sleeping boy's clothing. As they moved away from him, they took on three-dimensional form.

"It's no wonder they have been tearing you up," Kenny commented softly. "The scorpion and the butterfly hate each other. They fight for total control over you, and hate that they have to share. A fight for power is always ugly." .

The butterfly fluttered above the candle flame, while the scorpion advanced toward it, its stinger held high.

"Tamlin would not want this for his boy," Kenny muttered, "but it is Tim's choice."

Kenny made his way over to Tim, taking care to give a wide berth to the deadly scorpion. *What drove you to this?* he wondered. He knelt beside the sleeping boy, and shook him.

"Brace yourself," Kenny said, even before the lad had opened his eyes. "If they hurt going on, letting them go will hurt worse."

"Huh," Tim mumbled. He didn't want to have to be awake. Being awake was too hard. "Hurt?" he repeated. "What's going to hurt?"

"That all depends."

Tim was jolted awake by a strange sight. A butterfly and a scorpion circled each other in the center of the room, as if squaring up for a fight.

"Are those . . . are those my tattoos?" he asked.

"You don't recognize them?" Kenny seemed surprised.

"It doesn't seem possible."

"Why have you stunted yourself this way? I see the Wobbly may have been right. This is why it tried to collect you."

"What do you mean?" Tim asked.

Kenny gestured at the living tattoos. "By having these prison guards etched into your flesh, haven't you thrown away all of your potential? All that you are?"

"Is magic all I am?" Tim demanded, anger rising. "You don't know what it's like. I —aahhh!" A shooting pain in his chest caused Tim to howl in agony. *How can this be happening? The tattoos aren't even on me.* Through his squinted eyes he saw that the butterfly hovered over him, beating its wings frantically.

How can such a delicate, flimsy creature cause me so much pain? Tim wondered.

"You consented to their control," Kenny explained. "It doesn't matter if they are on your skin or not, as long as you have given them permission to be in charge. You and the tattoos have formed a link."

The pain subsided. Tim flopped back onto the pillow and used the rumpled sheet to wipe the sweat from his face.

"Why would you allow yourself to be caged?" Kenny asked.

"She said . . . she said they'd keep me from hurting someone," Tim explained, letting the sheet drop. "That's more important than anything else."

Kenny stood over Tim. "I could offer the same thing. I could kill you. That would prevent you from taking any actions at all. Everyone would be safe from you then."

"But—" Tim protested, sitting back up.

"Is this really the solution?" Kenny gestured at the scorpion and butterfly.

Tim perched at the edge of the cot and watched the strange creatures in their grotesque dancelike battle. The flickering candle flame cast their enormous shadows on the walls. *Depending on how you looked at it*, Tim realized, *things could seem much larger than they actually were*. The tattoos' shadows made them seem like monsters out of a horror film.

"These are artificial restraints," Kenny said, "but effective. The scorpion will sting itself to death rather than give up."

"Tell me about it," Tim muttered.

"Anything artificial is weak." Kenny crossed his arms over his thick chest and leaned against the wall. "Using something to step between you and your true self, as those do, well, that's never the most powerful choice."

"I know." Tim sighed. "I know." His heart thumped nervously as he saw the scorpion and the butterfly heading toward him. He wondered if they had noticed he was awake and were returning to their posts.

"Decide," Kenny insisted. "You have a moment now to decide."

Everything Kenny was saying made sense: that these tattoos were a false kind of security and that he'd still keep having to face everything that frightened him—with or without the scorpion and butterfly. But if he removed them, wasn't there even worse danger? Or was he simply taking an easier way out?

I want to be brave, Tim decided. *And I want to be strong. So I have to face the magic head-on, I suppose.*

Tim took a deep breath, wondering if he'd survive this next step. *What's that saying? Oh yeah, what doesn't kill you makes you stronger. I suppose I'm about to put that to the test.*

As Tim walked into the center of the room, the butterfly fluttered up to the rafters, leaving the scorpion scuttling across the floor. Tim leaped out of the way of the upraised stinger, nearly tripping over his own feet.

"Steady, boy," Kenny warned from the shadowy corner.

Tim decided he'd better rid himself of the scorpion first, since it seemed the most dangerous of the two tattoos. But how?

Tim circled the candle, keeping it between him and the scorpion. *First, I need to keep it away from me long enough to come up with an idea.* He glanced over at Kenny, hoping to get some assistance or a hint. The man's face was shrouded in shadow, his expression unreadable. *Man, I'd hate to play poker with that guy.*

No help from Kenny. Fine. So what do I do?

The flame from the candle sputtered as a bit of wax pooled in its center. The scorpion advanced again.

Fire. Most creatures don't like fire. Tim picked up the candle, dripping the hot wax onto his fingers.

He grimaced, but didn't allow the pain to distract him. *I sure hope I'm right about this*. He knelt down, bringing himself closer to the scorpion's stinging range, and waved the candle at it. Instead of running away, as Tim had expected, the action made the scorpion furious. It lifted its tail and attacked the candle flame with its stinger.

"Arggggggggghhhhhhh!" Tim howled. The flames quickly engulfed the scorpion, and as it did so Tim felt every lick of fire, every scalding scale. Finally, the agony was over, and Tim collapsed to the floor. The mangled, burnt corpse of the scorpion lay beside him.

Sweat coated Tim's skin, making him feel sticky and shiny. But he also felt more open, as if tight bindings around his chest had been removed.

"Whoa." The room spun as Tim sat up. He shut his eyes and breathed slowly. Gradually, he felt less woozy, and he opened his eyes again.

"You have done a brave thing," Kenny said from the corner.

Tim had almost forgotten the man was there, he'd been so silent.

"Some things must be done for oneself," Kenny said. "Although there is no shame in asking for help. Help simply may not come in the form you expect."

"Like you helped me see the tattoos clearly," Tim realized, "but wouldn't help me fight the scorpion."

A movement above him caught Tim's attention. The butterfly glided down from the top of the window and hovered near Tim. Up close, Tim was amazed by the delicacy of its wings, their translucent colors, the odd fuzziness of the insect's body. He held a finger up and the butterfly landed on it.

"Boy . . ." Kenny said warningly.

"Huh?" Tim's head whipped around, wondering if the scorpion had somehow come back to life. "What is it?" He didn't see any danger. Then he felt an itching on his arm. He glanced down and saw the butterfly's wings beating lightly against his skin.

"Hey!" Tim shouted, smacking at the butterfly. To his astonishment, instead of scaring the thing away, or squishing it, the butterfly flattened back into a tattoo—now on his bicep.

He glared at Kenny. "You distracted me. Now the stupid thing is stuck on me again."

The man shrugged. "You invited it back to you," Kenny replied. "You were not ready to let it go."

"But I was. I am," Tim protested. "I didn't want it, I just wanted . . . I don't know what I wanted. Just . . ."

"Do not kick yourself too hard, Tim. At least you stopped the thing before it returned to your heart. You will understand one day."

"How did you get the tattoos off me in the first placc?" Tim asked. He figured if he found out how Kenny had accomplished that, he could try getting rid of the butterfly later.

"I did not remove them. You did. In your sleep."

"Yeah, right," Tim scoffed.

"Things like that must leave you when you dream. When you dream, there is no room in you for lesser things. I gave them light, so they could see and hunt each other. That is all. Firelight. Because fire dislikes the unnecessary."

Tim puzzled over this. That would explain why the fire freaked out the scorpion. But he didn't want to have to burn the butterfly off his skin. And if it only left while he was asleep, he wouldn't be awake to destroy it. There had to be some other way. "How do I get rid of the one I've still got?"

Kenny stretched out his legs and leaned back against the wall. "Let me know when you find out."

Tim's mouth dropped open. "That's all you can tell me?"

The man shook his head. "No. I can tell you a

little more: You must learn to be honest with yourself. And more than that—accept what you discover."

Tim held his arm so he could see the tattoo better. "That's when this will this go away?" he asked.

"That will depend on you," Kenny replied. "The scorpion restrained your magic. This butterfly trains you to keep your emotions in check, so they will always operate at a lower pitch. Like a filter. No big lows, but no big highs either."

"Sounds calm," Tim said. "Which doesn't sound that bad actually."

Kenny sat back up again. "That kind of thinking is what led the butterfly back to you. You welcome its prison."

"Hm." Tim leaned against the bed, feeling done in. Not only had his experience left him physically exhausted, his brain felt squeezed, too. Kenny had given him a lot to think about. *This must be the kind of help he means*, Tim thought. *The confusing kind. The kind that only leaves you with more questions.*

He slowly got to his feet.

"You going somewhere, lad?" Kenny asked.

"I think you're right," Tim replied. "The only way I'll get a grip on this magic thing is if I face it dead on."

Kenny nodded. "And what do you intend to do?"

"Get some answers. Or at least, try to. I think to figure out who I am, I need to understand where I came from—how I happened."

"That's a way to begin," Kenny said.

"So I think I'll go have a little talk with Mummy Dearest. It's time to return to Faerie."

Chapter Nine

MOLLY O'REILLY GRIPPED THE pitchfork and tossed soiled hay onto the growing pile behind her. *Keep focused on your task*, she thought. *If you start thinking too much, you'll get angry all over again.*

"But I have a right to be angry," she muttered. "Grown-ups are complete dictators. Kids have no say in anything." She grunted and pitched another forkful of hay. *Fine, I broke my curfew and snuck out while I was grounded. They acted like I killed somebody! And I wasn't even with Tim, which was what they were so worried about.*

So now I'm in exile. Sent to Gran's farm out here in the country. Miles from London. Miles from Tim. Not even a chance to say good-bye.

Molly stood the pitchfork upright in the ground. She leaned on it, wiping her dark wavy hair away from her sweaty face. *As if Gran isn't a* _bad influence_, Molly thought, _with all of her fairy stories and so-called encounters with the wee folk. Though I guess I shouldn't scoff anymore_, Molly realized. _I've had close encounters of the weird kind myself lately._

Molly yanked the pitchfork out of the dirt, leaned it against the side of the barn, grabbed a bucket, and started pouring water into the horse troughs.

"Bless me, child, don't you ever slow down?" Molly's granny Fiona appeared in the barn doorway. "I get tired just watching you."

"Then don't watch me," Molly grumbled.

"None of that cheek," Gran warned. "I know you're unhappy about the situation, but that's no cause to be rude to one who's done you no harm."

Molly sighed. "I'm sorry, Gran. You're right. None of this is your fault."

Gran crossed to Molly and put her hands on both of Molly's shoulders. Gran was thick and short, no taller than Molly, so she could gaze deeply into Molly's eyes. Her lined face grew even more wrinkled as a frown creased her forehead.

"You're pale, lass, and out of sorts. Take Turnip out of the corral and go for a ride. Get some wind in your hair, color in your cheeks."

"I don't feel like riding," Molly protested.

"Are you telling me that you feel like doing all

my chores several times over? And moping the whole time while you do so?" Gran took a step back and laughed. "Why, if that's true, then you are more tetched in the head than I am!"

"I'm not!" Molly protested. "I just . . ."

"You want to keep busy, I know, gel. But there are ways and there are ways."

Gran turned away, leaving Molly puzzled. Did this mean that Molly was being ordered to go for a ride? Or did it mean that a ride was merely a suggestion, and she could go back to mucking out the barn?

She liked that word. Muck was exactly how she felt.

"All right then, lassie," Gran declared, picking up a knapsack she'd brought in with her. "Ready you are."

So it had been an order after all.

"I packed you a nice lunch and goodies for the fairies. Maybe they'll join you for tea!" Gran chuckled. "You should take your picnic up to Leanan Hill. There's wisdom up there." She left the knapsack in the doorway and trundled off.

"Fairies," Molly grumbled, picking up the leather knapsack. "Oof. That's heavy. I guess fairies are big eaters. Who knew?"

Molly trudged out of the barn to the corral. Turnip, a large bay mare, stood grazing, her tail whisking away flies. Molly dropped the knapsack inside the wooden fence, then clambered up and over it. She dropped down into the corral with a soft thud.

"Like a ride is going to solve my problems," Molly complained. "But do I have a choice?" she continued, her voice growing louder as she got angrier. "Oh, of course not. Darn Gran." Molly kicked a rock. "Darn all grown-ups!" she shouted.

Startled, Turnip whinnied and trotted away. "Darn you, too, Tim!" she called after the retreating horse. Realizing what she'd said, her face flushed. "Turnip," she said through gritted teeth. "I meant Turnip."

She stormed back to where she'd dropped the knapsack and rummaged through it. "Mmm. Let's see." She felt around until she found a carrot. "Brilliant. Gran, you think of everything."

She stood back up. "Turnip!" She held the bribe over her head and waved it. "Yo! Turnip. I've got a carrot for you. Carrot!"

The horse eyed Molly, then clip-clopped back to her. Turnip nuzzled her to get at the carrot, and Molly let the mare take it with her big teeth. She stroked the horse's velvety nose and thought of the beautiful unicorn that she had met with Tim.

Tim. She shook her head, as if trying to dislodge him from her mind, and led the horse to the fence where riding gear waited. She slid in Turnip's bit, and slung the saddle over her high back, tightening the girth. Placing a foot in a stirrup, Molly lifted herself up onto the horse. "Well, let's go, if we must." She jingled the reins, and pointed Turnip out of the corral and onto the road to Leanan Hill.

Why is Gran making me do this anyway? Molly wondered. *Dad would say it's because she's touched in the head.* Molly recalled some of the stories he'd told about Gran. Like all the times he'd come home to find her dancing around the house with a skillet, swatting at the invisible fairies. Whenever Molly's father was particularly angry at Molly, he'd warn that she was becoming too much like her crazy gran.

"If that's what constitutes the definition of daft, I suppose I am," Molly declared. "I've seen fairies. Well, not anywhere around here, and they weren't invisible like the ones Gran seems to do battle with. But I have seen them.

"Actually," Molly continued, "to be exact about it, I've seen people from the land of Faerie. I wonder if that's the same thing."

Molly felt a slight chill as the thick foliage of the tall trees created a canopy that blocked the sun. "If Dad really thinks Granny is such a loon, would he have stuck me up here with her? I don't think so."

The path wound its way through the quiet woods. As Molly listened to the birdcalls and felt the soft breeze ruffle her hair, she began to grip the reins less tightly. Tension eased out of her, the soft sway of the horse beneath her lulling her into something approximating peace.

Maybe Gran isn't so kooky after all, Molly thought. She considered trying to work herself back up into her bad mood, just to prove Gran wrong, but then decided that would be stupid. Even stupider than talking back to her parents after she was caught sneaking out again—which was how she landed here in exile. "One of those dumb things you do that doesn't hurt anyone but you," Molly said.

Soon she emerged from the wooded area and saw the large, mysterious stones that marked the top of Leanan Hill. She headed Turnip up the path. *It really is beautiful up here,* she noted. She breathed in the scent of heather and noticed that the grass sparkled emerald green in the late afternoon sunlight.

"Here we are," Molly told Turnip. She swung down from the saddle and took off the knapsack. The horse immediately began munching on the grass. "Enjoy your lunch," Molly said, giving the flank a pat. "I wonder what Gran packed for me, other than carrots."

She reached into the knapsack and felt . . . paper? Had Gran included a note? She pulled out an envelope. No, it wasn't a note; it was a letter from Marya.

Molly sat back against one of the tall stones to read, enjoying its warm solidity. The sun's warmth had been baked right into the rock, and it relaxed Molly's tight muscles even more.

There were stories about the stones on Leanan Hill. Some said they were put there back in the days of the Druids for their rituals. Others claimed that the stones actually *were* those same Druids, now transformed and lending power to the spot for magical workings. Gran had always told Molly the stones were people who had crossed the fairies. After seeing Titania, the Faerie Queen, in action, Molly could well believe it.

But right now the stone didn't feel like anything other than a good sturdy support. Something she was in serious need of.

Dear Molly, Marya had written:

I don't know how to tell you this, because I think you will be upset, but I also know I must. I ran into Tim yesterday while I was out walking the puppy, and he looked truly terrible. He was upset and admitted he was confused. After I left him, I realized that he knew the puppy's name was Daniel! I didn't figure it out at the time, but the only way for Tim to have known that was if he had somehow been there that night and saw the Body Artist work her magic. Which means . . .

Molly crumpled the paper, unable to read another word. She knew exactly what that meant. It meant that Tim had heard everything she and Marya had said. That he now knew all about what he might grow up to do. And he knew she was thinking of breaking up with him for it.

Molly dropped Marya's letter and covered her face. *He must feel so awful*, she thought. Tim felt things so strongly, and with all he was going through now, finding out that he might grow up to be evil—that he could become a dragon—might push him right over the edge. "And I'm not there for him to talk to," she murmured. Then a new thought chilled her. "Will he even talk to me after what he heard me saying? And can I be brave enough to talk to him?"

She pulled her knees up to her chest and hugged them tightly. Why hadn't she just been honest with him and told him all she knew when she had the chance? To find out this way was so much worse. Tears sprang into her eyes. "Poor Tim."

What must it have felt like to have overheard

that conversation? *Like betrayal, that's what.* To have to listen to someone you trust talking about abandoning you like that. A total stunner. And worse, he'd been given no way to defend himself to her. *And worse than that,* Molly thought, stacking up worse and worsers, *must have been hearing that he could grow up to be evil!*

Molly found herself standing, pacing. "I have to talk to him." *But how?* She stopped abruptly. *It's not like Gran's wired for telecommunication. She doesn't even have a phone, not to mention e-mail. And it's not likely that Tim will come strolling up the lane out here.* "I wish he would. Or I wish I could go see him."

Wishes. Didn't Gran always say you could ask the fairies for wishes? On the top of Leanan Hill, as a matter of fact.

She tried to remember everything her gran had ever told her, all those stories she had dismissed as, well, fairy tales. There were nursery rhymes and bedtime tales and strange little folk sayings, and now Molly scolded herself for not paying more attention. Still, she couldn't be too hard on herself. How could she possibly have known that Gran might have been on to something—that all those stories might be real? Or realish.

Molly thought about the little sprites Gran

had described, and then recalled Auberon and Titania, the King and Queen of Faerie. Were they the same species as Gran's little fluttering winged mischief makers? It didn't seem possible. Titania and Auberon hadn't seemed like the types to grant wishes, either. Gran's wish-granting sprites must be of a different order; related but different. Kind of like the difference between house cats and panthers.

"I think I'm supposed to make an offering," Molly recalled. "Maybe there's something in the knapsack I can use."

Molly stood and Turnip snuffled her elbow, perhaps in search of another carrot. "Hm." She gazed at the horse for a minute. "I'm not too sure how little fairy creatures feel about horses." She walked around the horse and gave it a sharp whap on the rump, shouting "Hah! Go! Go home!"

Turnip took the hint. The horse galloped down Leanan Hill and headed toward the woods. Molly stood with her hands on her hips, watching it go. "Granny's fairies had better be as real as Tim's," she muttered. "I'm going to be pretty cranky if I have to walk home without getting a few good wishes first."

Molly was bending down to look through the knapsack when she noticed the ring of toadstools in front of the stones. It triggered another

memory. "That's called a fairy ring," Molly said,
getting more excited. "Gran always warned me to
never sit inside a fairy ring or I'd end up kidnapped by the wee ones. Excellent. Now I know
where to put this offering—if I can find one."

She rummaged through the knapsack. *Gran
was very thorough in putting together this picnic. She
actually packed me a picnic blanket.* She pulled it
out and laid it over her knees, suddenly feeling
stupid. She sank back onto her heels and shook
her head. "How pathetic am I? I'm actually trying
to invite a fairy to tea so that it will grant me a
wish."

She placed the blanket in the center of the
fairy ring. "I'm sure glad there aren't any wit-
nesses up here. I'd never live it down." She eyed
the monumental stones looming above her.
"You're not going to tell anyone, are you?" She
laughed and shook her head. "And now I'm talking to rocks! I think I'm the blockhead here."

Gran was probably making it all up, Molly
thought, her hope flagging again. *Besides, fairies
probably don't like tea. They probably go for dew-
drops and flower nectar or something.*

Her fingers closed around a tiny object. She
pulled it from the knapsack and stared at it.

In her hand was a tiny, elegantly carved
teapot! Painted a pale blue, it was designed to

look like a flower, and it was just about the size of a thimble. And, Molly realized, once she opened the tiny top, it even had tea in it!

I guess Gran wasn't kidding after all. Molly carefully placed the delicate teapot in the center of the picnic blanket. She pulled out several beautiful flower-shaped cups and saucers, each painted a translucent pastel color.

Molly grinned, gazing at the pretty setting. She didn't usually like dolls and tea parties and such, but the flower set, complete with creamer and sugar bowl, was charming.

"Granny didn't pick you up at the corner store, did she," she commented. "Well, this is encouraging. Maybe there *is* something to this fairy tea party concept." *And*, she realized, *creatures who could drink from these teeny-weeny teacups would be awfully tiny.* Nothing to worry about there. "Folks the size of dragonflies I can handle." Molly knelt by the picnic blanket, trying to figure out what to do next. *Shouldn't there be some magic words or a ritual or something?*

While she pondered how to approach the fairies, Molly poured the tea. *Maybe I should just invite them to join me.* She cleared her throat as if she was about to make an announcement. "Uh, please do me the honor of joining me for tea," she declared to the open air.

Birds sang, crickets chirped, but other than that . . . nothing.

Well, that didn't work. Molly screwed up her face in thought as she tried to figure out a different approach. *Maybe they prefer something more formal. But it's not like I can mail out engraved party invites.*

The sun was starting to sink low on the horizon. Molly didn't want to have to find her way back in the dark. She racked her brain for any little bit of fairy folklore. What had Gran said would summon the "wee ones"?

Something about walking in a circle. Molly hopped up and walked around the picnic blanket, taking care not to trample any of the toadstools comprising the fairy ring. As she did, a remembered rhyme popped into her head. "Fair little folk, wee pretty ones, please join me at the setting sun."

Twilight! That's right. Gran said that was prime time for fairies. Molly walked around and around the blanket chanting. The vivid scarlet rays from the setting sun made the tea set glow. Molly chanted louder and louder and walked faster and faster until she worked up quite a sweat. Her walk became a run, the stones seemed to spin, and finally, she collapsed onto the grass.

Still nothing.

She sighed. "I'm so stupid. Whatever made me think that would work? How dorky can I get?"

A powerful breeze whipped up, scattering the tiny pieces of the tea set. "Oh no!" Molly sprang to her feet and dashed after them, not wanting to lose them. Suddenly she froze, as the air in front of her shimmered, and then, as if there were an invisible door, the air parted, giving Molly a momentary glimpse into another world. An enormous blue man with curved horns on his head stepped out from the other landscape. The air shut behind him, and the wind died down.

"It worked," Molly gasped, dropping the flower sugar bowl. "Only it worked really differently than I expected."

She had imagined a tiny creature with sparkly wings. She was not prepared for this huge, powerful-looking blue man. He wore clothes that a Shakespearean prince might have worn: velvet doublet and breeches, a flowing white shirt, and high leather boots. A purple cape fluttered out behind him.

I know him! Molly recognized the man as Auberon, King of the Fair Folk. She had met him with Tim when they had been confronted by the King's wife, Titania.

"Wow!" she exclaimed. "I summoned the King himself!"

King Auberon gazed at her for a moment, then laughed. "The king is not 'summoned,' child," he said, "certainly not by the likes of you."

Molly crossed her arms over her chest. "You're here, aren't you?"

Auberon smiled. "You are presumptuous. I come here when I need to escape my own world. Did you not see the signs?" He waved toward the stones and the ring of toadstools. "This is a fairy place. We come as we choose, not at your bidding."

"Oh. I guess that makes more sense," Molly admitted.

"Why were you trying to summon fairies, Earth child?"

"I—I needed to make a wish." Molly gazed down at her shoes and blushed. It sounded really dumb when she said it in front of someone who could actually hear her.

But he didn't laugh. "There is something so important to you that you would work rituals to achieve it?"

"There's someone who needs my help," Molly explained, encouraged by his taking her seriously. "Only I can't give it. Unless someone helps *me*. And since I'm stranded out here in the middle of nowhere, all I could think to do was to turn to the fairies." She eyed the seven-foot Auberon warily. "You don't happen to grant wishes, do you?"

"I can. Are you asking me for one?"

Molly's eyes narrowed as she thought this over. From what she could remember, things could get awfully tricky when doing business with magical types. "What's the trade-off?"

"That depends on the size of the wish."

"Hypothetically, if my wish were that I could be with Tim and talk to him right now, would that be considered big? Hypothetically, remember." Molly didn't want to actually state her wish until she knew what she was getting herself into.

"If I were to grant that wish, the price would be that you would have to agree to stay where I bring you."

Those terms aren't so bad. I don't mind staying in London. Of course, she reminded herself, *I'll get into even more trouble, since I'll have to explain why I left Gran's and how I got back to London. But it would be worth it.*

Molly's heart lightened. She had found a way after all! "Okay." She nodded. "I wish that you bring me to Tim so that I can talk to him, and I agree I'll stay there."

"Done."

Chapter Ten

TIM SLIPPED THE OPENING Stone back into his pocket and became aware of the butterfly tattoo on his arm. It tingled but didn't hurt the way it had before. "I guess my emotions aren't running so high coming here," Tim surmised. "And magic isn't forbidden to me anymore. That's useful to know."

He looked around. "I've been here before," Tim realized. "This is the Faerie market."

All around him, creatures of every description were hawking a multitude of wares. Colorful booths were set up so that merchants could display their goods; rough wooden tables and benches dotted the center of the market where customers could indulge in grilled meats, delectable pastries, and foamy drinks. Tim knew he could enjoy none of these treats: to eat food in Faerie would trap him there forever. As would accepting gifts, favors, and any other little tricks these deceptively pretty folk got up to.

"I guess I should have been more specific," Tim muttered. "Instead of asking to open a door to Faerie, I should have asked the Stone to take me directly to Queen Titania." *You always have to be so precise when making magic*, Tim thought. It was worse than answering essay questions on Mr. Carstairs' history tests.

Tim decided to stay away from the market, as appealing as it was. It was far too easy to be distracted or tricked there, and then he'd never find the Queen—or the answers he hoped she would provide.

He strolled into a clearing so he could concentrate, in case he wanted to work magic. Paths led in all directions, and it was up to him to decide which way to go. "If I were a queen, where would I be?" Tim said, gazing first one way, then another. He smirked, picturing Titania. "Out wrecking someone's life, most likely."

He shook his head. *Okay, get serious*, he told himself. *You came here for a reason, so quit stalling*.

The butterfly twinged, and Tim had to face the fact that thinking about seeing Titania filled him with a mixture of dread, anger, and fear. The woman claimed she was his mother. All Tim knew was that she had tried to kill him when he was born and had tried to either trap him or scream at him the few times he'd seen her since. But he wanted to find out more—about his magical lineage, about how he ended up with William and Mary Hunter, and what role Titania might play in his potentially turning evil and harming Molly. That was the most important question of all.

"Pick a path, any path," Tim muttered. He shut his eyes, trying to sense Queen Titania. *If she really is my mom, shouldn't I feel some connection?* He snorted a laugh. "Oh yeah, Tim," he taunted himself. "Lock right on to those major maternal instincts of hers and you'll find her in no time." The tattoo stung his arm, distracting him.

Plenty of kids feel alienated from their parents, Tim told himself. *They wonder if they're adopted. Or wish they were, at any rate. At least I'm totally normal on that score.*

The butterfly burned even more as he thought of how he had felt when he still believed Mary and William Hunter were his parents. Of course, he had known William and Mary all of his life. He'd only met Titania and Tamlin a few times. How could he feel connected to people who were little more than strangers? And who, in Titania's case, clearly detested him.

He took a deep breath. *If I keep thinking, I'm not going to start walking.* He shut his eyes and spun around. When he came to a stop, he opened his eyes and peered at the shady path leading out of the clearing. He stared at it a few moments, having no feeling whatsoever about the direction it led. He shrugged. "This is as good a path as any," he decided, and set forth.

"The boy is here," Amadan, the Queen's jester, informed Titania.

"I know," Titania snapped. "I can sense him." She tossed her long green hair over one shoulder and paced the marble portico behind her castle. "What else does he want to take from me now?" she fumed.

Amadan followed a few feet above her head, his tiny wings beating furiously to keep up with her. When the Queen was angry, she moved quickly. And she was very angry now.

"First Timothy Hunter caused the death of Tamlin," she declared. "His own father and my beloved! Then he nearly destroyed my esteemed husband, Auberon."

The flitling landed on a branch that gracefully bowed with the weight of delectable Faerie fruit. "One could also say that Tim saved your kingdom for you, and then returned your husband to you safe and sound from the mortal world," Amadan pointed out. "Tamlin's choice was his own."

"The child was not meant to live," Titania argued, ignoring Amadan's counterarguments. "I was betrayed by that nurse of yours. She was supposed to have killed him at birth. Obviously, she did not."

"You should be grateful," Amadan said, "for the sake of all Faerie. Tamlin brought the boy here and fulfilled the prophecy that a child of his would save this realm. What would have happened if the child had not survived his first few days of life?"

Titania shuddered with irritation. *Why is Amadan pressing this point? Why does he insist on my gratitude to the child who created an irreparable rift between me and Tamlin even before he was born?*

A nagging voice in her head told her this was not strictly true. There had been differences between Titania and Tamlin far earlier that had already begun to rend them apart. It hurt too much to think of her own culpability in their separation, so she focused her anger on Tim.

"He should not exist," she growled.

"His life force is strong," Amadan observed. "Schemes and battles and the dreaded manticore could not kill him."

"He does have power," Titania acknowledged. "Perhaps great power." She stopped pacing and crossed her arms over her chest, gazing unseeing across her lands. Her eyes narrowed. "Why is he here?"

Amadan fluttered after her and landed on the low marble wall that ran the length of the portico. "Could he be here to claim rights to the kingdom?" he suggested, peering up at the Queen. "He is your son, and he has saved the lands; he might want a place at court. There is no other heir, as far as we know."

"Auberon may have something to say about that," Titania responded tartly. "The line is determined through the father."

Amadan cocked his head. "Has Auberon changed toward you since discovering your . . . indiscretion?"

"Not at all," Titania replied, "much to my surprise."

Titania had expected dire consequences when she had to admit that she was Tim's mother: furious accusations, scenes, and arguments. But there was a single conversation. Auberon had simply stated, "So you lied. Your child was not stillborn. The child I had thought was mine."

"That is correct," Titania had replied. "But when I discovered the child was half human, I gave him to the midwife to be rid of him. I had no idea the child was still living."

"Why would you think that *this* Timothy Hunter was *that* child?" Auberon asked.

"I didn't. Not when I first met him. It was Tamlin who made me realize the connection."

"Tamlin told you Timothy was your son?" Auberon asked.

"The child saved Faerie!" Titania snapped in exasperation, wanting the conversation to be over. "Who else could he be? And look at his power!"

That had ended the conversation, and since then Auberon had not said a word. If anything, he seemed amused by Timothy's existence.

She shook her head, perplexed. "Auberon has changed since his time among the Earth folk."

She knew she was taking a risk confiding in Amadan, but where else could she turn? When Titania had first met the flitling, his sharp features and sharper tongue had been a source of amusement and often strategic counsel. He had a keen eye for what was hidden and was a clever, often wicked, observer of the fancies and foibles of the courtiers. But lately she found his cleverness too acid and his pointy face hard.

This is what I am reduced to. Spilling out my concerns to this scheming jester. She recalled the days when she herself had slipped into the mortal realm seeking solace and escape. It isn't the burden of the glamour-filled Faerie, she suddenly understood, but the position of ruler that created such distance between her and all others. *Auberon and I should be turning to each other. We are all we have.* Perhaps she could make him see that, if her husband would only stay by her side long enough. As long as Timothy Hunter didn't interfere.

"The delights of Faerie seem only to annoy or weary Auberon," Titania said wistfully. "This dissatisfaction was already present in him, but it has grown much worse lately."

"Yes," Amadan said. "King Auberon has been leaving the realm regularly. Perhaps one day he won't return."

Titania bent down to glare at Amadan directly. "Shall I have your tongue cut out?"

"No, no," Amadan said hastily, bowing and scraping on the wall. "I meant no disrespect. Of course Auberon would never seek to leave you. And his disappearance is not an event we would ever hope would come to pass."

"Remember who is the ruler here, Amadan," Titania warned.

"If Auberon stays away more than he stays home, wouldn't that ruler be you alone?"

Titania glared at Amadan's too-innocent expression and knew that he had an agenda here. For some reason, he felt he'd benefit if Titania were the sole ruler of Faerie.

The flitling was moving into dangerous terri-
tory, but at the moment Titania was not in the
mood to challenge him. "You don't understand a
woman's heart." Titania sighed. "I don't want to
win the kingdom only to lose the King."

"Not any more, you mean," Amadan said.
"Since you've lost Tamlin."

"That is quite enough from you!" *Insolence
such as this could not be tolerated.* She raised a
hand, ready to remove his mouth or spell him into
oblivion.

Amadan fluttered to a nearby tree branch.
"We were talking about the boy's motives," he said
hastily. "Until he moves, we will not know. My
counsel is to watch and be wary. He may turn out
to be an important ally. Or a treacherous enemy."

Titania nodded slowly. *The boy is either very
brave or very foolish coming here*, she thought. Was
he testing her strength and power against his
own? Or was he simply a boy, wanting to see the
woman who claimed to be his mother? She shook
her head bitterly. *Mother. Hah!* She could see
Tamlin's fiery defiance in Timothy Hunter, yet
nothing of herself. All she did see was danger.

Chapter Eleven

MOLLY KNEW THE INSTANT she opened her eyes that she wasn't in London; not even close. She and Auberon stood on a flowery hilltop under a tree bearing completely unfamiliar fruit. The sky above them was a bright royal blue, uninterrupted by the jagged skyline of London or the moody twilight she had left at Leanan Hill. A shining palace, colorful banners flying from its turrets, rose majestically above a crystalline blue lake. Lilting music floated on the fragrant breeze, as courtiers strolled on the lawn, playing unusual instruments. It was a beautiful sight, and it made Molly sick.

"You tricked me!" Molly O'Reilly fumed at the King of Faerie. "You told me you'd bring me to Tim!"

"I have," Auberon said. "The boy you seek is here. Welcome to Faerie."

Molly's stomach tightened as she put it all together. Tim had returned to Faerie. Probably to talk to the green meanie herself, Queen Titania— the woman who claimed to be his real mom. It all fit with what Marya had told her in the letter— about Tim's confusion, about his overhearing their conversation. *Poor Tim. He must be really upset if he's voluntarily sought out Titania. She's never been anything but terrible to him.* Molly felt worse when she realized she was part of the reason he'd taken this step.

Then her stomach lurched completely as she connected the rest of the dots. *If Tim is here, Auberon lived up to his end of the bargain.* Which meant Molly would have to do the same. She'd have to stay here in Faerie. Forever.

"Can this week get any worse?" she wailed. "First pink dinosaurs kidnap me. Then I'm grounded and forbidden to see Tim. Next thing you know, I'm packed off to the remote wilderness with my loony gran. And now—I'm trapped forever in stinking fairyland." She kicked a rock, which turned out to be some kind of hedgehog thing with wings. It unfurled and fluttered away.

"There are those who find the delights of Faerie enchanting," Auberon said, "its beauty, its sport, its riches."

"If you think it's so great, then why do you

keep coming back to our world?" Molly challenged.

Auberon smiled. "You have me there, child. You have a clear eye." He sighed. "You see, I have grown weary of this existence."

"So you figured you'd trap me in it, too," Molly said.

"You entered into the bargain of your own free will," Auberon countered. "I gave you very clear terms. You could have said no."

"I know." Molly sighed. "Tim warned me that things get all screwy with magical people. He wasn't kidding."

Auberon strode a few steps down the hill. "Look at those Fair Folk. Forever at play. Their petty intrigues, their beguiling glamours. Pah! They play at life itself."

"Which brings me back to my point," Molly said, chilled by the King's obvious distaste for his own world. "You're going to keep me a prisoner here, in a place you hate."

"Ahhh, there you are wrong." Auberon turned slowly and faced her. "I have a deep love for this world. It is in my soul. I am tired of what it has become. Or perhaps it is simply that, since my travels to your realm, I now recognize the difference between authentic experience and one shielded by magic."

He lifted Molly's chin with his blue finger. "I believe you can help me. You have fire. You are honest. I can see that. Perhaps we can reintroduce the raw, wild spirit that began this world."

He turned and gazed at the castle again. "Once, the Fair Folk were more like the Elementals," he explained. "We had the passion of Fire, the inspiration of Air, the moody power of Water, and the solidity of eon-forged Earth. But we grew afraid of our own untamed nature and domesticated it, submerging it beneath prettiness and complicated rules and feuds."

"Blah, blah, blah," Molly said. "So you're bored. And you're discouraged by your own evolution. Not my problem. My problem is Tim."

Auberon's eyes narrowed, and Molly saw anger flash across his face. "You are insolent."

Molly shrugged. She was already trapped in a magical world forever. What did she have to lose?

"Hey, you claim you want what's real and what's raw," Molly pointed out. "Happy to oblige. So listen up: You promised to take me to Tim and I don't see him anywhere around here. So if you won't keep your end of the bargain, I don't have to live up to mine."

"Not so fast, small one." Auberon held up a warning finger. "Your young man is in this world, believe me. He is on his way to the Queen. I—I don't choose to see her at the moment."

Molly smirked. The powerful king was nervous about seeing his wife. "Yeah, you two don't exactly seem to have the greatest marriage," she said. "You need to go on the *Jerry Springer* show or something to work it out." Molly laughed. "I think I'd actually tune in to that episode!"

"You have the capacity to amuse yourself, I see," Auberon said dryly.

"Well, Big Blue, you could begin by not taking yourself so seriously."

"Big Blue," Auberon repeated, a slow grin spreading across his face. "I like that."

We're wasting time, Molly thought. "Look. If *you* don't want to see the Queen, think about how much harder it must be for Tim, who she positively despises. I really need to see him. I think he's in danger here."

"Yes, she is dangerous," Auberon admitted. "Your Tim has greatly displeased her simply by existing."

"I know," Molly said. "Tim's in no shape to handle any more family drama. He's already had more than his share."

"You have great compassion," Auberon observed.

"For Tim? Of course I do," Molly said. "Don't you people care about each other here?"

"You may find the Fair Folk a bit more concerned about themselves than others," Auberon said. "The ability to feel other people's pain, or joy or fear, is perhaps the human quality I envy most."

"It must be a very lonely way to live," Molly said. "No wonder you sneak off every chance you get. And now *I* get to spend the rest of my life with a bunch of selfish, self-centered magical types?"

"I will protect you here, Molly," Auberon promised. "You can teach me much, I believe."

"Yeah, but what do I get in the bargain?"

"You get to stay alive."

"Oh, right. That." Molly crossed her arms. "Well, I'm not talking anymore until I see Tim."

Tim climbed onto a boulder, pulling his feet free from the soggy muck that was supposed to be a path. "Maybe I should have used a more scientific method of choosing a direction than spinning around," he mused. It had seemed pretty promising at first: The path led through a pretty grove beside a river, and he'd managed to avoid meeting any weird creatures along the way. But then it had quickly turned into a swampy, boggy mess.

His first guide through Faerie had warned him never to leave a path once you started on it. So Tim wasn't going to risk it—he'd found out the hard way the dangers of doing that! "But what if being on the path is worse than no path at all?" he moaned. His sneakers squished, the bottom of his jeans were muddy, and the overhanging trees and thick brush made it impossible to see where he was headed.

The whole time his butterfly tattoo burned and tickled and stung. Which was totally weird, because Tim wasn't feeling too much of any-thing—other than impatience with all the mud. It was as if the area he was in activated the butter-fly somehow. "Now that idea does make me ner-vous," Tim admitted. "You never know what kind of mind twister you're going to come across in these magical realms."

Titania leaned back in her throne, a smile spreading across her green face. The image of Tim faded from the sphere floating in front of her. *Silly boy*, she thought. *You have made things quite easy for me. You have put yourself on a very convenient path—a path I can work my magic on even at this distance. All the elements already exist in the Murky Wood that I need to keep you from ever arriving at my castle.*

She tapped the tips of her fingers together, thinking, planning. "I wish I knew what you wanted," she murmured, her eyes narrowing. "Very well. I'll give you someone to talk to.

Someone you can explain yourself to." She laughed a low, throaty laugh. "And if your companion breaks your heart, and your resolve, then so be it!"

She beckoned the sphere back to her and gazed deeply into it. She waited until Tim's image appeared clearly inside the glowing orb. "Yes," she intoned. "Just stay on that path. Someone will join you soon enough."

Tim perched glumly on the mossy rock. He ignored the dampness of his seat, just like he ignored his wet socks. He focused instead on the fact that he was lost. He had no idea anymore which way he had come. There were multiple paths leading from this boulder.

"I swear the trees move around while I'm not looking," he muttered.

A cracking branch alerted him that someone—or something—was approaching. *That's strange*, Tim realized. *Normally I'd have some reaction, like 'oohhh here comes trouble,' or 'oh joy, help is on the way.' But instead, nothing.* Tim bit his lip, considering this change in his personality. The answer dawned on him: The tattoo must be doing its emotion-flattening work.

Tim turned to see who was emerging from the thick woods. His stomach lurched and the tattoo went into overdrive, stinging and burning him. His eyes widened and filled with tears—from the awful pain of the tattoo as well as from the shocking sight.

Tamlin stood in front of him. Tamlin—as he had looked just before he died, sacrificing himself so that Tim could live.

"My son," Tamlin rasped.

Tim's eyes flicked back to the ground. He couldn't bear to look at the tortured body, the contorted face, the stringy hair, all indicating the agony of death. Tamlin had been a powerful, swashbuckling figure when they had first met. To see him now, like this, was awful.

"My son, what are you doing here? Why have you come?"

Tim couldn't speak, couldn't look up. Could only sit still, fighting against the pain from the tattoo and his confusion.

"Talk to me. Tell me—what do you hope to find in this land?"

Tim forced himself to face the man. The high cheekbones created deep hollows, making Tamlin's once handsome face skull-like. "Is this . . . is this place for the dead?" Tim asked. *If that's true, then, boy, did I pick the wrong path!*

"This is just Faerie," Tamlin said. "You came here on purpose. I want to understand why."

Tim's heart pounded hard. *Could I have been wrong?* he wondered. *Is it possible Tamlin survived? If that's true . . .*

A sense of relief flooded through Tim. If Tamlin hadn't died, Tim could find the answers to all of his tortuous questions right here. Right now. Without ever having to face Titania. He would be able to ask his real father all about his origins, his past, and maybe what to expect in the future. Most important, the burden of guilt over Tamlin's death would be lifted. They could finally truly know each other.

He had to find out for sure.

"I'm sorry, but I have to ask you this," Tim said. "Aren't you, uhm, dead?"

Tamlin swayed a bit, and Tim rushed forward to steady his father. He tried to hide his horror as he touched the cold, paper-thin skin of the man's hand.

"What do you seek here, son?" Tamlin asked again.

"How can you be here talking to me?" Tim asked, wondering why Tamlin hadn't answered his question. A terrible thought occurred to him. "Am I—am I dead, too?"

"Do you feel dead?" Tamlin asked.

"I—I don't feel much of anything at the

moment," Tim admitted.

"Why are you here?" Tamlin asked again.

Why does he keep asking me that? Tim thought. *Is he concerned something is wrong in Faerie again?* "Don't worry," Tim assured the man. "The manticore hasn't come back or anything." The manticore was the creature that Tim had killed in order to save Faerie.

Tamlin stared at Tim. "The manticore," he repeated.

Uh-oh. Maybe I shouldn't have mentioned the manticore, since the manticore's venom is what killed Tamlin.

"You aren't answering me, boy," Tamlin growled. "You won't tell me what you have come for. Why? Are you here to harm someone else? Who will die this time?"

"Wh—what? Tim stammered, his heart thudding hard, the tattoo burning. Why had Tamlin suddenly turned on him? A minute ago he had seemed concerned and weak. Now the man loomed over him, enraged.

"Look at what you've done to me," Tamlin roared.

"I didn't mean to," Tim whispered. "I didn't ask you to. I would have died just fine on my own." *Maybe it would have been better for everyone if I had.*

•

Better for Tamlin. Better for Molly. "Owwww!" Tim
clutched his arm as the tattoo stung and burned.

Tim fell to his knees in the mud.

"Yes. This was your fault," Tamlin raged over
Tim. "I should never have sought you out in the
mortal world. Finding you was my ruin!"

Tim tried to block out the horrible words—
they hurt more than any blows could. He covered
his face and tried his trick of counting, hoping the
numbers would calm him and drown out Tamlin's
furious voice.

He's never spoken to me like this before, Tim
thought. *He wasn't exactly friendly when we met, but
he's never shouted at me. And who asked him to
switch places with me when I was dying anyway? It
was his idea.*

"I didn't do anything," Tim screamed at
Tamlin. "You did! You made that choice, not me!
Don't blame me for your own act!"

Tamlin staggered backward and shattered
into a million pieces. The shards twinkled as they
fell, then disappeared.

Tim's mouth dropped open. "Huh?"

His heart gradually slowed to its usual pace,
and his breathing returned to normal. He stood up
slowly, his jeans completely covered in mud. He
wiped his hands on his pants. "He wasn't real," Tim
realized. "He was some freaky tortured figment

of my imagination." He glared at the tattoo. "I thought you were supposed to keep me from feeling stuff like that."

Tim looked around the gloomy, swampy area. *Well, you certainly chose a lousy path. Imaginary people seem to populate these woods. Better find a way out of here and fast!*

Tim started walking along a path that he hoped would lead him out of the swamp, still unable to get a sense of direction. He had gone only a few yards when he spotted a bizarre sight.

What's a wrecked car doing in these woods? Heck, what's a car doing in Faerie at all? It sat right in the middle of the path, so Tim had no choice but to approach it. It was either that or leave the path, and he figured he was already having a tough time in Faerie. He didn't want to make it any tougher by risking the off-path dangers.

Tim's stomach lurched. He recognized the car. And he had a sinking feeling that it wasn't empty.

"Dad."

Mr. Hunter sat slumped behind the wheel of the car, a bottle of beer in his hand.

"Ungrateful whelp," Mr. Hunter snarled at Tim. "I raise you as if you were my own boy, and how do you repay me?"

"I'm sorry," Tim said, his voice catching. *Get*

a grip, he scolded himself. *Remember, he's not really here. It's an illusion.*

"Your apologies mean nothing to me," Mr. Hunter said. "You run away from home and come to this . . . place. What do you want here? What do expect to gain by leaving your home?"

"I—I don't know," Tim stammered. His brain felt sluggish, thick. He couldn't come up with the responses he needed. Usually his mouth worked faster than his brain, which sometimes got him into trouble. But now his tongue felt thick and his thinking seemed to be slowed down, as if molasses had gotten into his brain's gears.

"You don't know?" Mr. Hunter repeated. "You don't know what you're doing here? Well, I know *this*! You've brought me nothing but grief. In fact, I'm never leaving this car again. Go on, leave me be! I'm sorry I ever cared for you."

He's not real, he's not real, he's not real. Tim chanted those words over and over as he worked his way around the damaged vehicle. He could hear Mr. Hunter—or Mr. Hunter's double—muttering the whole time.

Maybe this whole Faerie excursion wasn't such a hot idea, Tim thought. *Maybe I should use the Opening Stone and go back home.*

He felt around in his pocket and pulled out the Stone. Staring at it, he thought about the real

Tamlin. Tamlin had given him the Opening Stone. _He never would have done that if he didn't think I had the ability to handle it_, Tim realized.

Tamlin would never have turned back. Tim took a deep breath. _I can be brave, too. I just have to keep reminding myself that these visions aren't real._ He slipped the Stone back into his pocket.

"Hey, Tim."

Tim's head whipped around. Molly O'Reilly was sitting on the low branch of a tree, just a few steps away.

His breath caught. Could Molly have followed him here? he wondered. It was the kind of thing she might do; if she didn't hate him, of course. After overhearing her conversation with Marya in the park, Tim wasn't so sure if Molly would want to see him at all. Still, the girl in the tree sure looked like Molly. She seemed a lot more real than Tamlin or Mr. Hunter.

"Molly," Tim said, approaching the tree. "What are you doing here?"

"The question is, what are _you_ doing here?" Molly countered. "Why would you ever come back to this freaky place?"

"I—I needed to," was the only answer Tim could come up with. He studied Molly carefully. Magic could definitely fool a bloke; he'd learned that the hard way. Once again, he had trouble sensing anything, as if he'd lost his ability to read between the lines, to interpret.

"Is it really you?" Tim blurted.

Molly laughed, a full-out Molly laugh. "Of course it's me. Who else would it be?"

Tim shook his head, grappling with his sense of reality. This girl *seemed* like Molly, and he so wished it was her. The *real* her. "I tried to go see you," Tim said, "but they told me you'd gone up to your gran's. How did you wind up here?"

Now Molly's dark eyes grew hard. "That's your fault."

"My fault?" Tim repeated.

"You and your magic." Molly crossed her arms over her chest. "Your magic is dangerous. To me, to you, to the world, even."

Tim's mouth dropped open. He had no answer for her. Everything she was saying was precisely what he'd been saying to himself.

"Why I ever thought I liked you is beyond me," she continued. "Look at you! You're a wreck. Worse—you're weak and untrustworthy. A total loser."

That was the tip-off. The real Molly would never be so cruel. She might want to break up with him, but she'd be kind about it.

He covered his ears. "I'm not listening to you!" he shouted. He hurried through the brambles, the tattoo burning more and more.

He burst out of the dark woods and found himself at the edge of a meadow. He bent over, hands on his thighs, his chest heaving as he tried to catch his breath.

He lifted his head and there, in front of him, glistening in the brilliant sunlight, was a castle.

I guess I managed to get here in spite of myself, Tim thought.

Chapter Twelve

A CHILL RAN ALONG Titania's spine. The boy had made his way past the obstacles she had laid before him.

"The Murky Wood did not deter him," Amadan observed. "He has great fortitude, that one."

"Yes," Titania acknowledged. She waved away her spying sphere and stood up. "Now I need to decide how to proceed."

"It was clever of you to send the specter of Tamlin to try to find out why the boy has come here," Amadan said. "Too bad it didn't work."

"I didn't take into account his age, his lack of experience," Titania admitted. "He was distracted by the shock of talking to a man he knew to be dead. If Tim were more experienced, that would not have been so startling."

"None of the other illusions broke him either," Amadan pointed out.

Titania ignored the flitling and crossed to the floor-to-ceiling window. Afternoon light streamed in, bathing the throne room in a rosy golden haze. She could see the boy making his way across the meadow to the castle.

"I will receive him here. Then I will decide what to do."

"I'll bring him to you," Amadan said. He fluttered out the window.

Titania felt cold, despite the warmth of the sun filtering into the room. *I should not fear a child so*, she admonished herself. *But this one . . . this one is unpredictable, which means he is harder to control.*

Titania crossed her arms. Control was paramount. It was the primary tool of safety. Yes, Tim made her feel unsafe.

My reign is not secure while he lives. Amadan is right, the boy is too powerful—he could claim the throne. Or he could choose to come and live here, reminding Auberon daily of my infidelity. She knew having a child by another man was considered treason. Auberon could have her hanged for it, or banished, so he could marry another and have a legitimate heir of his own.

Tim Hunter was nothing but trouble. *He cannot live. I must find a way to ensure he does not.*

* * *

"So, we meet again," Amadan said, materializing a few inches from Tim's face.

Startled, Tim jerked his head back and swatted at the air.

"Hey!" Amadan scolded. "Watch it. I'm not a gnat!"

"Sorry, I thought you were something even more annoying. Like a mosquito," Tim said. "And if you don't want people to react like that, then don't buzz into their faces!"

"The Queen requires your presence," Amadan informed Tim icily.

"Oh, does she?" Part of Tim wanted to tell Amadan to buzz off. On the other hand, his whole purpose in coming to Faerie was to talk to Titania. So really, to argue with Amadan would be a self-defeating exercise in meaningless rebellion.

Tim gestured at his muddy clothes. "I hope she's not expecting anything formal."

"We're used to the indecorous ways of the humans," Amadan said.

"Oh, well, on behalf of us rude humans, we're grateful for your tolerance," Tim said sarcastically.

"Come along," Amadan ordered.

Tim followed the little creature through the meadow, across the bridge over the lily-filled pond, and into the castle. The enormous marble halls were lined with tapestries, and every few feet stood urns filled with flowers. It was light and airy inside, a striking contrast to the dark heaviness of the swamp.

"The Queen will receive you in the throne room," Amadan explained.

"Whatever." Tim's mind raced, trying to figure out what he would say, ask, demand.

"Timothy Hunter," Amadan announced, then flew out of Tim's way so that he could enter the room.

Titania sat on a tall velvet throne. Another, empty, throne stood beside her. *That must be for Auberon*, Tim noted. *I'm glad he's not here. This will be a lot easier to do with just Titania. Though I suppose Amadan never goes too far away.* He noticed the flitling perched on a nearby windowsill.

"Come closer, child," Titania ordered.

Tim stepped along the violet carpet leading to the platform that the thrones sat on. He had never seen Titania so formal before. She wore a glittering crown and flowing robes, and even held a golden scepter. *Should I bow? Aren't there rules when dealing with royals? Those rituals are probably a lot more complicated in Faerie.*

Oh, I don't care, Tim decided. He was worn out already, and he hadn't even begun to deal with this powerful and scary woman.

"Why have you come to my kingdom?" Titania asked. "You were not invited here."

"Actually, I came here to see you," Tim replied. *Might as well get straight to the point.* Then it dawned on him: She had asked him the same question that Tamlin, Mr. Hunter, and Molly had when he was lost in the wood. Could those illusions have been sent by Titania? He wouldn't put it past her. But it also meant that she was nervous about his being here. That made him feel a little braver.

"We have no business, you and I," Titania informed him.

"Right," Tim said. "Let's see, I believe you said you're my mother. I think that means we *do* have business."

Tim wasn't sure, but her green skin seemed to grow paler. He couldn't tell if it was from fear or anger. Another example of his inner sensors being out of whack.

"*I* decide such things, child." Her voice was calm, so maybe he was wrong.

I wish I could get a sense of what she's thinking, Tim thought. *But I don't seem to have very good radar.*

Hang on. That's not quite true. My gut instincts have only been off since the butterfly tattoo landed on my arm.

Stay focused, Tim reminded himself. "Why do you get to decide?" he demanded. "I have rights, too, you know."

Titania rose from her seat. "Not here, you don't."

"I don't care that you're a queen," Tim said. "If you have the right to show up in my world and threaten me, then I have the right to ask you some questions."

Titania's eyes narrowed, but she sat back down again. "What is it you want to know?"

"Everything!" Tim blurted. "What does it mean to be half Faerie and half human, for starters? And how did I end up with Mr. and Mrs. Hunter? What is this magic deal anyway? And why—"

"Stop!" Titania held up a hand and cut him off. "These are big questions with bigger answers. I must decide if you are worthy."

"Worthy?" Tim repeated. "What do you mean? Worthy of the truth?"

"Precisely."

"And how do you want me to prove that?" Tim demanded.

Titania smiled. "I will set you a challenge," she told him. "If you meet that challenge, you shall be told all you wish to know."

"What kind of challenge?" Tim asked.

Titania's golden eyes glinted. "A quest," she decided.

"You want to give me a few more details?" Tim asked. He knew from old storybooks, fairy tales, and myths that quests were usually undertaken by heroic types—and they didn't always end well.

"You come here in search of answers *from* me," Titania said. "So I shall send you to search for something *for* me."

She settled back into her seat and a small smile played across her regal features. Her expression sent shivers along Tim's spine. She reminded him far too much of a cat about to pounce for him to think this was a good idea.

"There is a jewel-encrusted goblet that once belonged to this royal house," Titania explained. "It was plundered during a war and is now in the hands of the graken."

Tim raised an eyebrow. "The who?"

"A creature with a spiny hide, poisonous fangs, and several heads."

Tim nodded, smirking. "Right. Of course. Wouldn't have expected anything easy."

Titania gazed at him, and once again Tim noticed that her eyes had the uncanny ability to change color. "Do not fear that I will send you on this quest unaided," she said, her voice now smooth and soothing. "Yes, it is dangerous; yes, many others before you have failed and thereby lost their lives."

"Is this your idea of a pep talk?" Tim asked nervously.

"Ahhh, but you see, I will work a binding on you," Titania crooned. "We will forge a link, so that I may counsel you wherever you are."

Something didn't seem right to Tim, even in his slightly addled state. *She wants to send me on a deadly mission, just to win the right to get answers to perfectly reasonable questions,* he realized. *On top of that, she wants to do a spell on me to connect us, claiming it would be in order to help me. That so does not add up.*

Tim glanced over at Amadan. The little flitling had a smug smile on his angular face. That clinched it. This so-called quest was some kind of trap. But if he didn't do as the Queen said, how would he ever find out what he wanted to know?

"Tim!"

Tim shut his eyes at the sound of Molly's voice. *Is this part of the challenge, too? Is Titania going to use another Molly clone to test me?* He took a deep breath, then turned to face Molly.

She stood in the doorway of the throne room, King Auberon beside her. *She looks like the real Molly,* Tim observed. But so did the Molly in the woods. And what would Molly be doing in Faerie anyway?

"Auberon, husband," Titania said. "I didn't expect you. And who is your . . . guest?" Titania's voice dripped with acid irritation.

Huh? This is a surprise to the Queen? Tim stared at Molly. *Could she be the real deal?*

"We've met before, Titania," Molly said, stepping into the room, "but you were a little distracted at the time. You were too busy being nasty to notice me, I guess."

Tim smirked. *That sure sounds like Molly.* Titania ignored Molly and spoke instead to Auberon. "You should teach your guest manners," she said.

"I would change nothing about Molly O'Reilly," Auberon replied.

"Molly, is it really you?" Tim asked.

Molly raised an eyebrow. "I come all this way, and you don't recognize your own girlfriend? Sheesh! Did Queenie magic you or something?"

"No, no!" Tim protested. "It's just—well, a lot's been happening."

Molly looked at him, and Tim could see her taking in his muddy clothes, his messy hair, and basic, to-the-bone exhaustion. "Yeah," she said. "I guess you've been going through a lot lately."

"Why did you come here?" Tim asked Molly.

"I thought you didn't want to have anything to do with me." He covered his mouth. He hadn't meant to blurt that out. Now she'd guess he had overheard her conversation with Marya in the park.

Molly grabbed his hands and squeezed them tight. "Tim, I'm so sorry. I should have told you everything. I—I was a total chicken."

"Don't be sorry," Tim told her. "It's okay. I understand. I would have been pretty freaked myself."

Molly looked him straight in the eyes. "I'm guessing you *are* pretty freaked."

It is so great to see her, be near her. But we still have so much to work out. Is that even possible? "Oww!" Tim dropped Molly's hand and grabbed the tattoo. It stung terribly.

"What is it?" Molly asked, her face furrowed with concern.

"The tattoo," Tim choked out.

Molly held Tim's arm and examined the butterfly. "You went and got yourself tattooed? What kind of bright idea was that?"

"I did it to stop myself . . . stop myself from, you know, doing bad things."

Molly stared at him. "How does a tattoo do that?"

"It's training me to stop having such chaotic emotions," Tim explained.

"What? That's crazy. You can't just shut off your feelings," Molly said. "That's the same thing as shutting off who you are."

Tim nodded. "I got rid of the one that stopped my magic. I don't know how to get rid of this one."

"That *is* what you want, right?" Molly asked.

Tim thought about that. He had to admit he was afraid of what would happen if he removed the tattoo. But it hadn't made his life any better—or safer for that matter. In fact, cutting off his emotions had made him more vulnerable, since it also blocked his instincts, his intuition.

"Tim, you have to be a whole person," Molly said. "I like all of you, not just the calm parts. Stop feeling and you become worse than these two." She gestured at Auberon and Titania. "That's why Big Blue is so miserable—he wants his real feelings back. As for her"—she nodded toward Titania—"her real emotions must be so buried she barely knows happy from sad."

"Yet she does know anger, child," Titania warned. "And you have tried my patience long enough. Your insults! Your interruptions!"

"Leave the children alone," Auberon said, "or you will have me to deal with."

The tattoo burned and stung as Tim battled with himself. Could he risk being totally himself again? Wouldn't that mean that he was endangering Molly?

"Come on, Tim," Molly said. "You know I'm right."

Tim smiled through his pain. "You usually are," he admitted. "Okay, I'm willing to lose the tattoo. But I have no idea how to do that."

Molly held his arm in both her hands and studied the butterfly. Tim liked the feeling of her soft fingers, of being close to her again.

Molly bit her lip. "People do get tattoos removed. I think it's like tattooing in reverse."

"Trust me," Tim said. "That's not the way I can get rid of this thing. I've had a little experience with these thingies."

Molly nodded. "Yeah, magic never works the way you think it will." She smiled at him. "We'll figure out how to undo this little mistake. The important thing is that you _want_ to be rid of it."

Tim smiled back. It felt good to have Molly on his side, even if the tattoo hurt more the happier he felt.

Molly ran her finger lightly over the tattoo, tracing its shape. "Can't you magic it away?" she asked.

"I got rid of the other tattoo by fighting it," Tim said. "But I don't think that's going to work with this one." He thought back to that bizarre night with Kenny. He shuddered. "And the tattoos seriously fight back."

"What if you wished really hard?" Molly suggested. "You know, kind of how you made those little narls and Awn the Blink appear. You could make the butterfly *dis*appear."

"I—I don't know if I can." He gazed down at the ground. "I think I'm afraid of how much it's going to hurt," he admitted softly.

Molly took his hand, straightening out the arm with the tattoo. She placed her other hand just above the butterfly. Her brow furrowed, then she looked at Tim. "Think of it like pulling off a Band-Aid. It stings like crazy, but then it's over. Just concentrate, like this."

She laid her hand over the butterfly and gazed into Tim's eyes with fierce concentration. He could practically feel her wish boring into his brain.

He smiled at her. "I get what you mean. I'll try."

Molly grinned, then removed her hand. To Tim's astonishment, the butterfly fluttered off his arm.

"Wh-what?" Molly stammered. "How did that happen?"

"You did it!" Tim cried. "You removed the

tattoo!" He threw his arms around her, letting his heart expand with happiness and relief.

"What did I do?" Molly said. "I don't understand! Is magic contagious?"

Auberon stepped up to them. "Tim may be the Opener of Worlds, but you, my child, are *Tim's* Opener. You allow him to open up to energies but, more important, to himself."

Tim turned to face Titania. Now that the tattoo had been removed he could think clearly again.

"You know what? I don't think I should have to prove my worth to my own mother," he informed the Queen. "I'm not going on any quest for you."

"Then you will never learn the truth," Titania warned.

Tim's jaw set. He hated giving up the opportunity to find answers to his questions, but he knew it was wrong to have to be tested in this way. Knew it in his gut.

Auberon stepped forward. "There are other ways to learn the truth," he said. "My queen is not a reliable source for you."

"Then coming here was a waste of time," Tim snorted.

Auberon cocked an eyebrow. "Was it really?"

Tim looked from the King to Molly. "No," Tim

whispered. He took Molly's hands. "No, it wasn't wasted at all."

Molly ducked her head, hiding her blush. Tim had never seen her this shy before. Then again, they hadn't ever been together like this in front of Faerie royalty.

"Let's go home, Molly," Tim said.

Molly's grip grew tighter, and her expression was stricken. "I—I can't," she stammered.

"What do you mean?" Tim asked.

"I made a bargain with Auberon. In exchange for bringing me to you, I had to agree to stay where he brought me. Which turned out to be Faerie."

"Oh, Molly!" Tim gasped. He couldn't believe that she had made such a sacrifice.

"Please," he begged Auberon. "She's not magic—she didn't understand how these things work. I'll stay in her place."

"No way!" Molly jumped in. "It was my mistake. I should have known better. Now I have to accept the consequences."

Auberon looked from Tim to Molly. "No. You belong together. She is your Opener. And neither of you belong here. I see that now. I will send you back."

"Really?" Tim was incredulous. Then a darker thought blotted out his relief. "What's the catch?"

"No catch," Auberon assured him. "What you two share is real. And," he added with a nod to Molly, "I am seeking a more truthful reality. You belong together. So, Molly, I release you freely from your bargain."

"Thank you," she said gratefully. She grinned at him. "You're not so bad, once a person gets to know you."

Auberon smiled. "I hope we will continue to know each other better, Molly. I grant you both free passage in Faerie." He snapped his fingers, and when he opened his hand two small coins sat on his blue palm. He passed his hand over them, and Tim watched tiny sparkles surround the coins, then settle onto them. *He must be charming them*, Tim realized.

"These are not gifts," Auberon declared. "They are tokens to carry with you, signifying you are under my protection in this realm."

"Sort of like passports or visas," Tim said as he took the tokens. He handed one to Molly.

"With these, you can come and go as you please," Auberon said. "Alone or together."

"Together," Tim repeated. "Do you know what that means?" he asked Molly.

"A new way to break curfew?" she replied mischievously.

"You don't understand," Tim said, his smile

growing along with his admiration for Auberon. "Time passes differently here. We could spend a week in Faerie and no one back home would even know we were gone! Of course, we'd have to make sure to bring our own snacks, since we can't eat Fairy food."

Molly returned his smile. "We can see each other without getting into trouble!"

"Exactly." Tim shook his head. "I don't know how to thank you," he told Auberon.

"You already have. You released me from entrapment before; I am only returning the boon."

"I guess magic *can* solve some problems," Molly said, turning her glittering coin over and over in her hands.

"Are you ready to return?" Auberon asked.

"I am now," Tim said. *Now that I know I'll be able to see Molly again any time we want.*

Molly's face grew concerned. "Are you really?" she asked Tim. She glanced up at Titania, who was sulking on her throne. "You don't want to ask her anything else?"

Tim raised an eyebrow. "You really think she'll answer me?"

"Nah," Molly agreed. "She's too busy pouting."

"As I said," Auberon told Tim, "there are many ways to discover the truth. I would seek it elsewhere."

"Get them out of here!" Titania shouted angrily.

Tim took Molly's hands. "See you soon," he said. He pulled her close to him and kissed her. Right there in front of the King and Queen of Faerie. And he didn't even feel shy about it.

Chapter Thirteen

TIM FELT MOLLY'S HANDS disappear from his. "Molly!" he cried. He opened his eyes and saw that Auberon had returned him to London—alone. Tim assumed Molly was back at her gran's farm. He'd be sure to check on that as soon as he figured out how.

But the first question on his mind was why Auberon had sent him to the cemetery—to Mary Hunter's grave, in fact.

"Wow!" Tim gaped at the large, sprawling bush that had sprung up out of the grave. When Tim had been at the brink of death, Death herself had given him some seeds. He had planted them at the grave of the woman he had believed was his mother. This bush was what had grown from them.

He stepped closer and discovered the bush was covered with intensely deep purple berries. He'd never seen anything like them before. His stomach rumbled, and he realized it had been days since he'd had anything to eat. Should he risk eating the berries? They could be poisonous—or worse, magical in some unpredictable way.

His mouth watered. They looked really juicy and sweet and he was so hungry. They hadn't grown in fairy soil but in Earth dirt. That was encouraging.

His stomach rumbled again. "Oh, just go ahead," he told himself. "If Death were trying to kill you, she wouldn't need berries to do it." Feeling a slight twinge of anxiety, he plucked a berry from the bush and popped it into his mouth.

The world changed in front of him. It was as if he were suddenly taller, and he no longer stood in front of a gravesite. He was in a rose garden.

He reached to pluck a rose and discovered his hand was not his own. It was slender and wore a bracelet. *A woman's hand.*

Weirder and weirder, Tim thought. And then his own thoughts vanished, replaced by someone else's.

What a pretty flower, she thought. She pulled it to her, taking care to avoid the thorns, and inhaled the scent deeply. She snapped the bloom from the bush, and worked the rose into her hair.

"A fair flower for a fair maiden," a voice said behind her.

She whirled around, hoping she wouldn't get into trouble for taking the flower. A man stood in front of her. A man like none she'd ever seen.

He was tall and slim with long straight hair that hung softly around his chiseled face. He looked like a movie star or someone on the telly. He was dressed like an actor in one of those BBC costume dramas. Thick, chocolate brown leggings revealed shapely legs; tall boots and a long leather coat gave him the appearance of a swash-buckling adventurer or a pirate.

She realized she was staring, and blushed. She quickly dropped her eyes to her shoes and waited for him to speak again. She didn't trust herself to speak. Not only had he taken her breath away, she was sure she'd stammer something foolish.

He took a step toward her and smiled. "I am called Tamlin," the man said.

His voice thrilled her. It was rich and reso-nant, and he sounded so refined. Not like her rowdy neighbors in the council flats. "I—I'm Mary. Mary Cavanaugh."

The image faded, as if a movie had ended. Tim jerked back into consciousness. He felt faint from the astounding experience. "That was my real father, Tamlin. And my—my— Mary." Tim knew that Cavanaugh had been Mary's name before she had married Mr. Hunter. *But I was seeing it as if I were her!*

He stared at the bush. *The berries. I ate a berry and I had one of Mary's memories.* That answered one question—how Mary and Tamlin had known each other. Maybe there were other answers, too. Tim grabbed another berry from the bush and ate it.

He was in a new place. He was Mary again, and she was sitting on a blanket in a thickly wooded grove with Tamlin. It was autumn now; roses had long since been out of season. The nearby river rushed across boulders and stones, adding a subtle music underneath their serious conversation.

"I know you are keeping secrets," Mary said. "Trust me enough to tell them to me."

Tamlin stood and gazed across the river. "How can I burden you with my problems? The mistakes I made were made so long ago I don't know how they can ever be undone."

"Please, I see how troubled you are." Her voice was soft and gentle. Tim could feel her sympathy for the struggle she sensed in Tamlin. He could feel her trust in the man and her intense, overwhelming love.

Tamlin turned and faced her again, his expression sad, his eyes glistening with unshed tears. "Until now, I had not mourned the choice I

foolishly made so long ago. I had times of joy and
times of great sorrow and anger. But never once
did I regret. I didn't mind the velvet chains that
imprisoned me. You see, I had left nothing behind
that could claim me. That was until I met you."

He knelt down and took her hands in his. This
time Tim could feel how much this man loved
Mary. It flowed out of his hands into hers, like an
electrical current, like the river to the sea. "I will
tell you everything. I am done with dishonesty. I
am done with foggy visions and cloudy experiences. I want truth and truth alone. So I will tell
you."

Mary nodded, a twinge of fear momentarily
fluttering her heart. She squeezed his hands.
"Truth is what I want."

Tamlin sank back on his heels and gazed long
and hard at Mary. He seemed to be preparing himself for the possibility that once Mary heard what
he had to say, he'd never see her again. "I know
you have already guessed that I don't live here,"
he began slowly. "Not in this world. I live in the
land called Faerie."

"You mean like in storybooks?" Mary asked.

Tamlin smiled wryly. "Not *un*like. But far
more lovely—and far more treacherous."

"Does that mean . . . you aren't human?" Mary
asked. Tim was shocked that she felt no fear as

she asked this, only curiosity and concern.

Tamlin stood. "I am as human as you are. But I left this world when knights were still battling for honor and warring clans killed one another, fertilizing their lands with the blood of their enemies."

Tamlin watched her expression carefully, and Mary forced herself to keep the astonishment from showing on her face. Perhaps it was this struggle or the tension of the moment or the extraordinary unreal reality she was now facing, but she began to laugh. Tamlin was perplexed.

"How do you find this funny?" he asked.

Mary gulped in air, gasping for breath. "I always wished for a knight in shining armor," she choked out. "I never expected my wish would be granted so . . . so _literally_!"

She wiped the tears from the corners of her eyes and smiled up at him. "And I never saw myself with an older man either. Certainly not a suitor several centuries older."

Tamlin knelt down and embraced her. "You are a delight. And extraordinary."

She let herself fall against his chest for just a moment, taking in his solid reality. What she was hearing was so bizarre, she needed the reassurance. She sat back upright and took a deep breath. "Go on."

Tamlin released her. "Yes. My story."

He stood again, and couldn't seem to look at Mary as he spoke. "I took a walk one night and came upon a beautiful woman, weeping as though her heart would break. She was the Queen of Faerie herself, though I did not know it at the time. By my own free will I accompanied her to her realm, which made me her prisoner."

"You mean you were never able to return home?"

"Never for very long," Tamlin replied. "It was a good enough life, I suppose." He turned to face her again. "But now you see why we cannot be together. I am bound to the Faerie realm and its Queen. I can give you nothing, not even myself—you, who deserve everything."

Mary leaped up and flung her arms around his neck. "I don't care," she sobbed against his chest. "I don't care about any of that. I love you, and I know you love me. We will steal what moments we can."

Tamlin gently pulled out of her embrace. "My sweet Mary. You say that now. But you will care, care deeply. It will eat at you, each time we part, just as it will eat at me. You deserve to have a true husband, a family. None of which I can offer you."

Mary trembled in his arms, fighting back her frustration, her sorrow, her anger. "It's so unfair!

Isn't there some way to break her spell? That is," she added quickly, stepping away from him, "if you could be happy returning to this world after all your time in Faerie."

"A world with you in it is a world I would be happy in," Tamlin said.

That was all Mary needed to hear. She gripped his hands. "Then we have to try! We have to try to find a way to keep you here!"

"I have heard legends and stories," Tamlin said slowly, then shook his head. "I don't know if I believe them."

"Anything that will help us! What do the stories say?"

Tamlin bit his lip and narrowed his eyes, remembering. "There is an old tale the balladeers sing. On Halloween night at midnight, the Fair Folk ride through the mortal realm. I've done this myself. It is said that at that time any creature under the thrall of the Faerie Queen may escape through the trials of a true love."

"A true love," Mary repeated. She smiled. "That's where I come in. This might work."

"It will be quite difficult," Tamlin warned. "Queen Titania does not relinquish power easily."

Fear crept into Mary, no matter how hard she tried to ignore it. "What kind of trials will I face?" she asked, her voice quavering a little.

Tamlin stroked her hair. "You must pull me down from the horse that I ride at the first stroke of midnight. You must hold me until the final one has sounded."

"That doesn't sound so hard," Mary said.

"The Queen will fight you," Tamlin explained. "She will transform me into all sorts of beasts. She will try to harm you through me. But if you don't let go, I will be yours."

"I'll do it."

The image faded.

Tim had to find out what happened next. He tossed another berry into his mouth.

It was cold and dark. There was no moon, making it darker still. Mary paced by a willow tree at the edge of a meadow. An enormous ring of toadstools circled the meadow—Tamlin had told her this was the sign of the spot at which they would enter from Faerie.

Tim could feel both Mary's fear and her resolve. She shuddered against the cold wind, terrified she'd fail and afraid of what she would face. But she was determined to win Tamlin his freedom.

She started at the sound of tinkling bells. Her mouth dropped open as the air in the center of the fairy ring rippled and an enormous golden horse slipped through what seemed to be a slit in the atmosphere. The horse stamped the ground with its front hoof, then whinnied and reared on its hind legs, as if it were announcing its presence.

As glorious as the proud horse was, it could not compare with the exquisite, haughty beauty of its rider.

She is every inch a queen, Mary thought. Queen Titania seemed to be made of moonlight; everything about her shimmered, twinkled, sparkled. Even the moonless night sky glowed brighter around her. She wore the same flower garlands twisted through her long hair as those braided in her steed's mane and tail.

And yet, Mary thought, smiling, *Tamlin chose me, plain Mary Cavanaugh from Birmingham, over that astounding and powerful beauty*. Pride filled Mary with courage. She was ready.

"Join me!" Titania cried. Dozens of horses and riders appeared. The horses pranced inside the fairy ring as their riders sang in a language Mary could not understand. If so much didn't depend on her, if there were nothing to lose, the scene before her would have been enchanting. Instead, the lovely melody, the gorgeous people on their decorated horses, all made the situation seem more deadly. *Like roses with thorns*, Mary observed. *Such beauty comes with a price.*

She spotted Tamlin on his milk-white

mount—just as he had told her he would be. She knew she had to wait until the correct moment. Everything had to be done according to plan. Tamlin had been quite clear about that. Magic followed rules. If she deviated from the rules, all would be lost. But if she followed them to the letter, Queen Titania would have no choice but to release Tamlin.

She checked her watch. The hands were approaching midnight. She made certain she was in position to reach Tamlin quickly. The Queen's horse was at the other side of the circle, facing away from Tamlin. *Thank goodness for that at least*, Mary thought. That would give her the few seconds she needed to get to Tamlin before the Queen noticed.

Yes! The first chime of the clock tower sounded and Mary raced out of her hiding place. She gripped the horse's bridle, then dragged Tamlin down from his horse. He could do nothing to help her; the rules dictated that she was stealing him from the Queen. She released the horse and clutched Tamlin to her tightly.

"Be brave, my darling," he whispered in her ear.

Another chime sounded as Tamlin's horse shied and broke from the orderly circle. The Faerie courtiers had trouble keeping control as the riderless horse galloped erratically among them. What had been an orderly procession dissolved into chaos.

"Who has broken the circle!" Titania demanded furiously.

"Tamlin is off his horse, Queen," a tiny, fluttering creature cried above the noise of the whinnying horses and shouting riders.

The bells chimed a third time.

The Queen rode her horse into the center of the circle. She pulled it to a stop a few feet from Mary and Tamlin.

"Who interferes with my courtiers? Who dares to defy me?"

"Don't answer," Tamlin instructed Mary. "Stay focused on me. On our love. On our future."

Mary shut her eyes tight and took comfort in his solid presence. Then that solidity began to change as the bells rang again.

His arms released her, and she no longer embraced a tall, strong man. A thick, wriggling, cold creature squirmed in her arms. She opened her eyes just as an enormous snake opened its mouth and flicked its tongue at her. She shrieked, and she had to struggle to keep her grip, but she held on.

It must be twelve feet long, she realized, straining to avoid its deathly grip. Its head bobbed around, as if it were looking for a place to strike. *It's so heavy, and slippery!* Mary's arms burned from the effort of hanging on to the flailing creature. Every time she thought she had it in a secure hold, a portion of its long body slid out of her arms. It hissed and writhed and tried to wrap itself around her. And still she clung to it, wondering if she'd lost count of the bells. Was that three? Or was it four?

The snake reared its rubbery, boneless body away from her, preparing to strike. As it moved its head toward her, it transformed.

Into a lion!

Mary stared into the enormous gaping mouth filled with sharp teeth as the lion let out a roar and the bells chimed once more. She was too terrified to scream. Keeping her arms around its neck, she ducked down and around. She now gripped the lion's mane from behind, and no longer had to see that terrifying face. The lion began to buck, trying to shake her off. She knit her fingers more deeply into the golden fur. *My fingers are too weak*, she thought, beginning to panic. *I won't be able to grip much longer*. With a burst of energy, she scrambled up onto the lion's back, so that she could cling to him with her whole body. Another bell chimed and Mary felt panic rising. She'd lost count. Could it only be

chime number six? Was she only halfway there?
Time itself seemed to have slowed down.

The lion roared again and twisted around
trying to see her, to bite her, to shake her off. And
still Mary held on.

"You're winning," a small voice said in
her ear.

Startled, Mary nearly lost her grip. A tiny
creature with sharp pointy features and rapidly
fluttering wings flew at her shoulder.

"You're doing well, human," the creature said.
"Keep at it!"

Mary shut her eyes, forcing herself to concentrate on not letting go. But she appreciated
this tiny cheering section. Perhaps this little fairy
was also a prisoner of the Queen's. Maybe she
could save him, too. But for now, she had to focus
on the chimes and Tamlin. *That was eight*, she
thought. *And again: nine.*

The lion let out another bellowing roar, then
transformed once again—into fire!

"Aghh!" Mary shrieked. The flames licked at
her, singeing her flesh. The heat seared her eyes,
but she could see that what she held wasn't
just fire but Tamlin himself in flames. He was
burning up!

"Water!" the little voice beside her urged.
"Douse the flames and you'll save him."

The clock tower rang again. Surely the ordeal was almost over.

Mary looked at Tamlin's features, contorted with pain inside the column of fire. *The river!* She had to save him. She dragged the burning Tamlin toward the river as the chimes sounded once more, feeling blisters forming on her hands, her arms. She crossed out of the fairy ring and jumped into the rushing water just as the bells chimed again. *Twelve*, she thought with relief.

The moment they hit the water, the current pulled them apart. The cool water soothed Mary's burns, and she knew it must be doing the same for Tamlin. She burst up through the surface and gulped in air. "Tamlin!" she called. Where was he? She whipped her head back and forth, peering into the dark night, trying to find his beautiful face above the water.

"Tamlin," she cried, fear chilling her more than the water. "Tamlin!" Could he still be under-water?

With a sound that sent horror plunging through her heart, the clock tower chimed one last time. That's when Mary realized she would not find Tamlin in the water with her. She had not held on to him through the last chime of midnight. She had failed.

"And you were so close," the little fairy

creature taunted from a nearby tree branch. "You really should be careful whose advice you take, human."

Mary swam to where she could stand and stared at the creature. "You tricked me."

"You were willing to be tricked," the fairy retorted. "As I said, you should check your sources. I am Amadan, the Queen's jester. Why would I do anything to help you do her harm?"

Mary gazed back up to the fairy ring. Tamlin was slouched on his white horse, glowing ropes wrapped around him, a gag in his mouth. Mary noted that even his eyes were covered, so that they could have no contact at all.

Titania glared at Mary. "You should take care, mortal. I am not one to cross."

She gave an order, and the invisible doorway between the worlds opened once again.

Mary scrambled out of the water and up the bank to the meadow. "Tamlin, I'm sorry! I love you, Tamlin!" Mary cried.

She could not tell if he heard her or not; he simply disappeared through the door with the other riders. The Queen placed her horse directly in front of Mary. She peered down imperiously.

"This is over," the Queen declared. "You will never see him again. I will create bindings that will prevent any further contact between our realms. Forget him." The Queen galloped her horse around the fairy ring three times, then it leaped into the air. At the height of its jump, the horse and rider disappeared.

Mary sank to the ground and sobbed.

The image faded.

Tim found himself on the ground, shaken from Mary's ordeal and engulfed in the pain of her separation from Tamlin. It took him a few minutes before he could stop himself from sobbing Mary's heartbroken sobs. Finally, he sat up and leaned against her headstone.

"How horrible," he murmured. *How sad for them both*. No wonder Tamlin seemed so angry and sad inside. While Mary was ashamed that she had failed and devastated that Tamlin was gone forever.

"It wasn't your fault," Tim told the headstone. "Titania cheated. She used Amadan to trick you."

He didn't want to leave this experience yet. He needed to reassure himself that Mary had found a way to be happy. Though it was hard for him to imagine she'd found that happiness with William Hunter. And he wanted to know—how had he come into the picture?

He ate another berry. And found himself as Mary, talking to a much younger version of a man Tim knew well: William Hunter. A Mr. Hunter who still had both his arms.

"It will be all right," Mr. Hunter said to Mary. Tim could feel tears trickling from Mary's eyes.

She wiped them away quickly. "I just feel so stupid. I'm sorry. I shouldn't bother you with my problems. But you've always been such a good friend to me. I didn't know who else to turn to."

"I'm glad you did. Having a baby isn't so hard. Lots of people do it." He gave her a little smile. "Even hopeless cases like you who've never learned to cook or clean or anything useful."

Mary laughed. "You're such a jerk," she teased.

"That's why you like me."

Mary dabbed her eyes, and her shoulders slumped. "I'm just so afraid. I knew my parents would be disappointed, angry even. But I never thought they'd throw me out."

"They'll come around," William Hunter offered.

"No, Bill," Mary replied. "They won't. Besides, I'm an adult. Twenty-five years old. This is my responsibility." Her voice began to tremble again. "How am I going to manage on my own?"

She started to really cry, and Bill put his arms around her. Mary burrowed into him, seeking comfort, and Tim felt her relaxing in the safety of Bill's company.

"You don't have to be alone," Bill said softly. He cleared his throat. "Mary, you know I've always loved you."

"I love you, too." She rested her head against his shoulder. It felt cozy and safe.

"I know you care for me as a friend," Bill corrected. "But I love you with all my heart. And I want you to be my wife."

Tim could feel that Mary had strong feelings for this man. They were completely different from what she had felt for Tamlin. Those emotions were fiery and filled with passion. What Mary felt for Bill was softer, gentler, and much calmer. Tim could sense her fear melting as she considered his marriage proposal.

Then a cold shiver went through her.

"It wouldn't be fair." She shook her head. "I can't. You deserve someone who will love you with all her heart and soul. I do love you—but not that way, you're right."

William took her hands in his. "I know you still have feelings for the mysterious father of your baby. But you've made it very clear that he is never coming back. Isn't that right?"

Mary's eyes lowered and she nodded.

"Then why not make a go of it with me?"

Mary bit her lip. She did adore Bill—he was her best friend. They had fun together and they could talk about everything. Well, everything but Tamlin. Maybe her fond affection would grow into something deeper, with time. "If you're sure . . ." she said, still uncertain if she was doing the right thing.

Bill smiled. "I think we will be great together. You even laugh at my jokes!"

Now Mary smiled back. "You're right. You'd better marry me while I still think you're funny." Her face grew serious again. "Bill, let's move. Let's go to London, where no one will know this child isn't yours."

"Whatever you want."

The image faded.

Tim couldn't stop now. He had to see all the memories that the bush was offering. He found a cluster of berries and popped them all into his mouth.

This time it was like watching a montage; it must have been because he'd eaten so many at once. Mr. Hunter—Bill—helped Mary get up from the couch, while she was very pregnant. Mary gazing wistfully at a full moon, touching her swollen belly. "Tamlin," she whispered. "I will take good care of our child." Exhaustion and great joy while holding her newborn in a hospital bed; Bill beaming and crying, overwhelmed by emotion. "Let's name him Timothy," Bill suggested.

The images faded. Tim felt completely drained. He had experienced so much in such a compressed time. It was like watching one of those sports roundup programs on telly: Tim got the highlights only, all of the most intense bits.

"That baby was me," he realized slowly. Tamlin and Mary Hunter *had* had a baby together. *And that baby was me. Titania isn't my mother after all!*

This must have been what Auberon was trying to tell me, Tim thought. *This is why he returned me to this spot. So that I would learn the truth. How did he know?* Tim shrugged. *Must be one of those magic things. Maybe he could tell that I was all human, while Titania was so blinded by what she thought she knew that she didn't notice.*

Everything had happened the way Mr. Hunter had told Tim. He had married Mary when she was already pregnant by another man. Whatever child Titania had with Tamlin, it wasn't Tim. The child the Queen of Faerie had gotten rid of must have met its own fate.

"Wow," he murmured. "I may have a half brother out there somewhere. The child Titania thought I was—her son and Tamlin's." He wondered briefly why Titania had been so convinced she was his mother, but he pushed aside those thoughts as bigger, more important realizations entered.

No one tried to give me away. In fact, Tim thought, a lump forming in his throat, *my mom and dad—Mr. William Hunter and the former Mary Cavanaugh—really loved me. A whole lot. Even Tamlin, I suppose, loved me in his own rough way. Why else would he have sacrificed himself for me?*

And, of course, Molly. Molly who risked so much to help him. *Even Auberon helped me find the answers I needed and found a way for me to see Molly.*

Magic can help after all. Go figure.

Tim stood and gazed for a long time at his mother's grave. Funny how spending time as someone else—first the cat, then his mother— had helped him learn so much about himself.

He felt sad all over again, missing his mother and also mourning for what she'd gone through, but for the first time in a long time he didn't feel so lonely.

Staring at the grave, an idea came to him.

"There's something I need to do."

Chapter Fourteen

TIM MADE HIS WAY to the car a few blocks from his flat. He stood and stared at the wrecked car, finally understanding its allure for his dad. It was the last place they'd been together, Bill and Mary. And it was the source of all his dad's pain. His loss. His failure. Everyone said the accident had not been his fault, and yet Mr. Hunter had never forgiven himself. The car was the reminder of all that. As long as he continued to come here and sit in it, he would be trapped in that pain and guilt forever. It hurt too much for him to move forward without Mary.

It sickened Tim to see the vehicle. It always reminded him that people you counted on could disappear for no good reason. But today had made him realize that help could come from unexpected places, and new people appeared as the need arose.

He hated the car; hated how it caged his dad in pain. *Like the tattoos*, Tim realized. Freedom took many forms, Tim had learned, and required several steps. Tim had taken many of those steps since discovering he was magic. He felt he could help his dad take one now.

"Wobbly!" Tim called. He shut his eyes and focused on the scavenger, willing it to appear. "Wobbly, the Opener is summoning you." There was a pause, then the beating of wings and a rush of air over his head.

"Krawwwwwww," the Wobbly cawed. "Opener, you have need of me? Has been long time since you called."

Tim noticed the Wobbly had grown into a sprawling cloud of garbage. "There is something here for you," Tim told it.

"You have not thrown anything away," the Wobbly complained. "Where is the useless? Where is the thing for recycling?"

Tim pointed at the car. "There. It's all yours. It's the least useful thing I've ever seen."

"Then I shall take, Opener."

Tim watched the creature grow until it was large enough to clutch the ruined car in its talons. It gripped the car tightly and lifted it into the air. Tim watched until the creature and the haunted car vanished beyond the horizon.

Tim felt instantly lighter. The past—at least that horrific frozen moment of the past—was gone. It had happened; nothing would ever change that. But now it wouldn't drag them down and hold them there with it.

I hope Dad feels the same way, he thought with a momentary pang of anxiety. *Well, what's done is done.*

"This was a good thing to do, even if he doesn't realize it at first," Tim decided. *Let's see, should I tell him I got rid of it, or just keep quiet and let him discover it's gone?*

"Nah," Tim declared. "Truth is best. I'll tell him it's been taken away for salvage." *And now we can salvage ourselves.*

Tim turned to leave the car park and saw a familiar figure slowly approaching. Mr. Hunter—the dad he had grown up with, who had raised him even though he knew that Tim wasn't his child, who had loved Mary with all his heart, was slowly pacing his way toward the lot. A few yards from Tim, Mr. Hunter looked up.

"Tim," he said, astonished. "What are you doing here?"

"I . . . uh . . ." Tim wasn't sure how to explain his mission at the parking lot, or how he had accomplished it, so he let his words trail off. He wasn't even certain how much time had passed in his world while he had been in Faerie.

Mr. Hunter studied Tim's face, his expression concerned. "Are you all right, son?" he asked. "I know I was short with you a little while ago. Out of line, really. But you had me so worried . . ."

His words trailed off, too. For a moment, Tim and Mr. Hunter looked at each other. Finally, Mr. Hunter's eyes flicked past Tim and scanned the lot. Tim saw confusion cross his dad's face.

"Where's the car?" Mr. Hunter said.

"Right," Tim said. "The car. Well, I kind of got rid of it." Tim braced himself. He wasn't sure how his dad would respond.

"You did?" Mr. Hunter asked.

"It seemed like the right thing to do," Tim explained. "That car was like a trap. Like quicksand. Dragging you down and keeping you down there with it."

Mr. Hunter stared at Tim. His eyes grew larger and Tim could see tears forming. _This is bad_, Tim thought, feeling a little panicked. _I won't know what to do if Dad starts to cry._ "Besides," Tim said hastily, trying to lighten the heavy moment, "this way you'll have to get me a car that I can actually drive. Once I hit sixteen."

Mr. Hunter nodded, blinking hard. "Maybe you won't be grounded by then," he said, his voice gruff and thick with emotion.

"You think?" Tim said, a grin spreading across his face.

"So what do you say?" Mr. Hunter said. "Ready to come home, Tim?"

"Ready as I'll ever be," Tim said.

And he meant every word.